ᴖter 1

Amelia strode purposefully and fearlessly.

She had reached the point where nothing else mattered. The outcome was as irrelevant as the danger, because the only thing that mattered now was to put an end to it all.

For it to be finally over.

The endless hoping. The years of uncertainty. The life lived with a leg in each camp. Never fully committing to either. Always waiting for fate to dictate her path but today, as she marched towards that car, she wasn't waiting for fate to tell her how her life was going to be. She was about to meet it head on. To deal with whatever lay ahead and to take control of her own destiny.

Unfaltering, she marched with unshakable courage because, before the sun would set tonight, one way or another, she would be free of uncertainty, of insecurity and of doubt.

She would be on her way to a new life with Frank and their daughter or she would have finally let him go, and her old life with Brian, Frankie and her family, would be enough. More than enough.

As Frank's silhouette came into view, she could already feel the relief of it. Like a soldier marching into a final battle, she had the comfort of certainty that soon, good or bad, her anguish was about to end.

She steadied her pace and approached the passenger door with more composure. She was already anticipating his initial reaction on noticing that Frankie wasn't with her.

She opened the door and he simply smiled widely.

"Did you forget something?"

"What?"

"You were meant to be heading home to get things sorted. Are you going or what?

She put her confusion aside and simply accepted his own. He'd obviously fallen asleep without realising and it worked in her favour.

She studied him closely. The colour of his skin, the way he moved and spoke. It all seemed as it should. He looked and sounded as normal as anyone else but still, she needed to tell him of the horror she'd encountered. Of the year that had passed in the blink of an eye. Three hundred and sixty-five days had 'been and gone' in the few minutes she'd sat in that car.

"Frank. I need to tell you something."

She watched his expression change to that of a man who was already bracing himself for devastation.

"You've changed your mind." He sighed.

"No. It's not that."

"What then?"

"When I got home, everything had changed. Frankie was at a sleepover; Brenda was back from London and I'd been reported missing!"

He laughed.

"You haven't even had time to get home and back! What's this about Amelia?"

"I'm telling you. Something strange happened today. Something strange and unexplainable."

He didn't reply

WHERE ARE YOU?
Part 2

3 HOURS

**Cover design
By KO Productions**

"Frank. I think this thing we have between us. This ability to get into each other's heads is a lot more than just a mind-reading trick. I think it's somehow holding us together."

"Well, if it is, I like it" He smiled.

"No. I mean, holding us together……against nature."

"What's nature got to do with it? You're not making any sense Amelia! What's this really about?"

She could feel his anguish.

"Look Frank." She just needed to get it all out. "I'm not lying. A full year went by while we sat here! It's ludicrous I know but our daughter is six now, not five! I can't make any sense of it!"

He saw her fear. This wasn't some ploy to get out of leaving with him. She was terrified!

He'd been feeling strange himself. The blinding headache had sent him nauseous, and he'd been hoping to use the time while she was gone, to grab himself a cup of coffee and an aspirin, but he hadn't even had chance to start the engine. She turned the corner and then reappeared in less than a second. She couldn't possibly have been home and back yet there she was, marching back with this story about a missing year!

He could feel the hope from her. She wanted him to disprove her rantings. To come up with a rational explanation they could laugh at, but he couldn't because he too, knew that something was wrong. Very wrong.

A few seconds ago, he'd tried to turn the key in the ignition but seemed unable to. It was as though his hand had no strength. He could see his hand on the key but when he tried, nothing happened. He'd tried to ignore it but now it felt like pieces of some horrific jigsaw were slotting together.

He studied her face. He tried to read her thoughts.

"You think there's something wrong with me, don't you?"

"I don't know. Maybe. How do you feel?"

"Honestly?"

"Honestly."

"I feel grateful that you're here, but I feel tired. So very tired. Like I haven't slept for weeks. Like I just want to close my eyes for a minute."

Her gentle smile betrayed her grief.

There was nothing she could hide from him now.

"You think I'm dying, don't you?"

She tried to smile again.

"But if you thought I was dying you'd be rushing me to a hospital, wouldn't you?"

She nodded and wiped away a tear.

"I don't think we are going to Australia tonight, do you?"

She shook her head.

"I think it's too late. I think something already happened to you." She whispered.

He frowned for a second and then he gave a little nod and sighed.

"I think I'm supposed to be somewhere else by now darling, don't you?"

She nodded again. Tears flowed down her cheeks as she cupped her hands around his face to draw him close, but her hands had no grip on him. Her fingers folded around his cheeks but all she could feel was a slight denseness as she watched them merge into the contours of his smiling face.

"Oh God, Frank. I'm so sorry."

"Don't be. I knew the risks. It was a gamble. These people are smart. Smart and determined, and at least I'm getting the chance to talk to you. That's a blessing. I have no regrets."

"How can you have no regrets? You've lost everything."

"My only regret is that I didn't get to meet our little girl, but I will. One day.... I will, won't I?"

"Yes, you will." She sobbed as she reached up to touch his face again.

She watched her hand circle his cheek, but she couldn't feel his skin. Her hand could feel the pressure of the outline but not the texture of it.

Her mind relaxed into him. She needed to feel what he was feeling. She could feel his sorrow, but he wasn't afraid. He was tired. So very tired.

She watched his eyes become heavy and she could feel it too. That unfightable need to let go of consciousness and just sleep.

She lay her head against his chest.

"You can sleep now Frank." She whispered. "I'm right here."

She closed her eyes to tune in again. To enter his mind and comfort him in those final moments but suddenly a different voice screeched into her ears. The impact caused her to open the eyes she hadn't even realised she'd closed. The sound of that voice wasn't even recognisable, but instantly, she felt the very essence of the little girl it belonged to. This was Frankie!

"Mummy! Mummy! Where are you? Please come back. I need you. Mummy! Mummy! Come back!"

Suddenly she was sitting bolt upright. As stiff as a poker and totally paralysed.

Her eyes shifted right and left in panic. Slowly she felt her brain regaining control of her body and she turned to Frank who was still lolling on the window with his eyes closed.

"Frank?"

She put her hand out to rouse him, but he didn't react.

She felt the dread, but it wasn't the dread of being unable to wake Frank. It was the dread that she might have fallen asleep.

She looked at Frank's watch. It was four o'clock. She sighed her relief. That was the same time she'd arrived at the car.

Perhaps Frankie was on the lane looking for her! Perhaps everyone was!

She recalled the voice again. She knew it was Frankie, but it sounded distorted and deeper. Something in this place was distorting and changing everything and she had to get out!

She remembered her science teacher saying that the supernatural is only supernatural until we understand it, then it becomes natural and no longer feared but this was something else. Nothing about this was ever going to feel normal. Whatever was happening was terrifying and every instinct was telling her to run.

She gave Frank one final, futile shake, but she knew he was out of reach. Frank was on a journey of his own now. A journey she couldn't share.

"Goodbye darling. I love you and I will see you soon."

She jumped out of that car and ran as fast as her shaking legs could propel her, but it was like wading through treacle as she thrust each leg forward with all her strength without making more than a few inches of progress. Something was pulling her back, and another level of terror had her in its grip.

She pushed and gasped without daring to let up for a second for fear of being catapulted back to that car.

Frank wasn't going to let her go! She thought of little Frankie's desperate cries, and her determination multiplied by tenfold! She had to get home. She had to!

Suddenly she lurched forwards. Catapulted several feet into the free and gentle air of normality. Whatever had been holding her had released her from its grasp.

One day she would reflect on that moment and realise that she had passed through some strange barrier of separation.

A threshold from which very few mortals have returned.

She collapsed onto the ground and gasped for air. Something colossal had just happened and no scientist was ever going to convince her differently.

A day ago, she scoffed at the suggestion of an afterlife, and at her father's notions that their mother was watching and wating for him, but today, she was in no doubt that there was something beyond this world. A place where they would all meet again someday and strangely, somewhere amid her terror, lay an element of comfort in that.

But today was not her time and she had only one person to thank for saving her.

Her little girl had somehow managed to connect with her and muster the power and strength to jolt her from that fatal sleep. Frankie had somehow called her back from the brink of this mortal world by the sheer desperation to find her mother.

It was time to go home.

She had done everything she could for Frank and now she could return to Frankie and Brian and put every bit of her love and devotion into securing their happiness.

Frank was no longer the nagging hope inside her, the shackle holding her back from compete emersion. One day, there would be a time for Frank. One day he would meet and love their daughter, but that time was not now. Not today.

Today, she was going to march back into her life with the enormous gratitude of having survived the battle.

Chapter 2

As she turned onto the street, her whole body began to shake and tremble. She recognised the symptoms. She was going into shock. Her body was reacting to the trauma in the only way it knew how. It was shutting down but, just like a shellshocked soldier returning from the battlefield she was marching home on autopilot. If she could make it home, she would be alright. There would be time enough for recovery and reflection. For support, understanding and compassion but first she had to get there. This was the final push. The last mile. Soon her ordeal would be over.

In front of her, a young man was ambling along. If she kept the same distance between them, she would be home in a few minutes. She just had to keep putting one trembling leg in front of the other.

She uttered a prayer. A bargain. She would be a devoted wife and mother if only she could walk back into her life to find nothing had changed. She would never yearn for Frank again if she could just slip back into that bed unnoticed and wait for the wonderful reunion with Frankie and her father.

She was still muttering her prayer when the young man in front of her started to talk. He was alone and still walking but he started to talk as though he was having a conversation with an invisible person! He wasn't muttering a quiet prayer but talking loudly to someone who wasn't answering. She immediately dropped back to put some distance between her and the mad man!

He turned onto the next street, and she felt the relief of it.

But her regained composure was short-lived as she approached the last curve in the road.

The wooden bus shelter had turned to glass!

A surge of dread rose through her body and crashed back down like a colossal tidal wave. There was only one explanation.

Another year had passed!

She swallowed hard and continued her course.

Every possible scenario was speeding through her brain and her legs no longer felt capable of carrying her, yet she was still moving. Had Frankie arrived home to find her missing again? Deserted for another year? Was she now seven! "Please God, no! Please, please, no!"

Had her father returned from Scotland to a family drenched in suspicion and anger? Had Sheila been forced to tell them everything? Of her selfish obsession with the boy from school? Of her adultery and her total disregard for Brian and the family they'd built together.

Then her mind returned to the biggest dread of all.

Frankie.

Two whole years of waiting for her mummy to return.

Those final moments with Frank could never compensate for the misery she'd caused to her trusting little daughter.

She thought she was doing the right thing, but she'd been so wrong. Wrong and stupid!

Her regret turned quickly to anger and then to resentment. She chose Frank over Frankie! Her lover over her child! And it was to be her downfall.

She took the corner into her own street with the desperate hope of some kind of redemption, but the sight caused her to falter.

Where are you? –Part 2   Three Hours

The entire street was strewn with cars. Lots of them. Parked nose to tail, straggling pavements and wedged into front gardens. She'd never seen so many cars crammed into one street.

She walked more slowly now. Almost gingerly. Anticipating some terrible event or confrontation but the car-littered street remained calm. The chaotic spectacle lay quietly dormant. As though resting or laying in wait. Preparing to pounce!

She turned up her path and tried to open the front door, but it was locked.

The front door was never locked in the daytime, so she assumed Brian and Frankie were out somewhere.

She peered through the window and then jumped back as a face appeared at the other side. The face of a man she didn't recognise.

She was still staring at the window when the front door opened.

"Can I help you?"

The man's tone was irritable and sarcastic.

His thin, middle-aged face with bulging eyes was wedged in the small gap between door and frame as his bare leg held back a small dog from escaping.

"Hello? I said, can I help you?"

She was lost for words. Her body refused to stop shaking but her brain was frantically processing the situation. It was obvious that this man lived here now. Brian must have moved out. Maybe taken Frankie and moved as far away as he could get from his unfaithful, selfish wife. Somewhere she would never find him!

"I.. I was looking for someone. He used to live here. Well, I used to live here as well actually. Brian. Brian Gilbert."

The man's eyes widened a little. Without taking them from Amelia, he called behind him.

"Anna! Get yourself out here."

There was a short silence in which he tried to smile politely. Amelia frowned questioningly.

"The wife knows more than I do." He added before giving his leg another unnecessary shove against the dog. "Get back Bruce."

"What is it?" Amelia asked impatiently.

"Anna! Are you bloody coming or what!"

He rolled his eyes at his wife's sluggishness.

"It's just that we were given a note to hold on to when we first moved here in case someone turned up."

Amelia's heart refilled with hope.

"I can't remember the name though. Sounded more like a flower than a name to me." He laughed apologetically. "What's your name?"

"Amelia." She whispered hopefully.

"That's it! Amelia. - Anna! It's that woman they said might turn up!"

At last, the illusive wife appeared behind him and pulled the door fully open, allowing the disinterested dog to sit quietly in the open doorway. She was of a similar age but still quite pretty despite the lines around her eyes and lips on that elfin face. A face framed by the straightest blonde hair Amelia had ever seen. It looked like she'd steamed it on the ironing board.

"Amelia?" She asked excitedly.

"Yes. That's me."

"Just a mo. I'll go get the envelope. We left it behind the gas meter, so it didn't get lost."

"You've been away then?" The man asked as casually as one might ask someone with an obvious suntan.

"Yes, I have. I didn't know he was planning to move."

The man just nodded as his wife's arm appeared over his shoulder waving the dirty retrieved, envelope from behind the gas meter.

"Thank you." Amelia smiled as she took the lifesaving envelope in her trembling hand.

"You're welcome." The woman smiled again. "I hope everything works out."

The door closed and Amelia was left standing at the wrong side of it. Homeless.

She squeezed by the car that had been rammed into the tiny front garden and sat on the same wall she'd spent so many hours on as a child.

She stared at the unopened envelope with it's stains and smears. Terrified of the contents.

There was every chance that it was a warning to stay away. A threat born of Brian's anger and pain. A note to leave her in no doubt that she was no longer welcome in their lives.

She turned it over and over as though the contents might be revealed more gently through the protection of the dirty envelope.

She continued to fondle it. Trying to enjoy these last moments of uncertainty. To hold back the tidal wave of devastation and allow hope to live a little longer, but the agony of uncertainty felt even worse than the impending desolation, so she quickly tore open the envelope and unfolded the small note.

'Cherry Blossom House, Station Road.'

She turned the note over but that was it.

Hope hadn't just offered her a glimmer but thrown open the curtains and let the sunshine beam in!

She knew that house!

She hoped it wasn't a sick joke.

'Cherry Blossom House' was the house that she and Brenda used to covet as children when they went out on their bikes with a jam sandwich and a bottle of water.

It was just under a mile away, set back from the road with a circular drive around a large Cherry Blossom tree.

They would lay their bikes beside the tall iron gates and peer through the railings at the big bay windows and make up stories about the family and furniture inside.

Inventing huge four poster beds, playrooms with rocking horses and of ballrooms with sweeping stairs on which they could hide and watch the adults. Just like in The Sound of Music.

Their fantasies were an escape. The re-creating of a happy family life that they no longer lived, after the death of their mother. They immersed themselves completely in it, dulling the pain, resurrecting their mother and everything she brought to their lives then elaborating it beyond reason. A perfect family in a perfect home with a mother and father who loved each other and who loved them too.

As they balanced their bikes with nettled legs and gabbled their fantasy stories, they were recreating something they'd once had. Happiness.

They would then turn their bikes around and wipe the tears across their sunburned faces before racing home as fast as they could to dull the pain of it all.

Amelia carefully folded the slip of paper and pushed it into her pocket before starting her journey in the direction of Station Road. She hoped desperately that this note was not just some sentimental reminder from Brenda of their pact to one day live together in that house. A reminder of the desertion of their childhood promises.

If more disappointment lay ahead, she desperately needed a fallback plan.

Before making the turn out of the village she veered in the direction of Sheila's.

Sheila would be able to enlighten her. Sheila would be her salvation. Just as she always had been.

As she approached the three bedroomed semi, she felt instantly comforted. The small front garden looked the same with hints of Barry's sense of humour. Imitation squirrels hung from the brickwork and a collection of garden gnomes huddled in the corner with their wheelbarrows, spades, and bare bottoms.

The hint of a tiny smile arose inside her, but it didn't manage to battle its way to her lips.

She walked down the pristine path, knocked loudly on the door and stood back with the certainty that her ordeal would soon be over.

After a few seconds she knocked again and then again. She peered through the window into the tidy living room with its new sofa, carefully folded newspaper and fringed rug and felt even more certain that this house did not belong to strangers.

Desperate to make some kind of contact with Sheila and Barry she sat on the wall for the longest time, but no-one returned.

Eventually, comforted that at least she had a place to come back to, she walked back out of the gate.

Wet, cold and hungry, she continued in the direction of Station Road. To the fantasy house of her childhood and hopefully, the place where she would be reunited with her family.

As she walked, she was already imagining the huge arched door with the dappled glass panels that distorted the images of the things inside. Just like the house of mirrors. She imagined the blurred but unmistakeable figure of Frankie approaching. The raven hair that would now be even longer. The petite little shape that might now have grown or thickened out even though she'd sat beside that little girl only this morning and watched her finish off a milk shake with just three sucks of that flattened straw.

The colossal magnitude of the incredible events she'd endured in just a few short hours imploded again. Fragmenting her brain into isolated pieces of logic that screamed their refusal to accept that any of this was real. Yet still those pieces were already re-joining and reforming themselves back into the hideous, crooked picture before her.

The impossible had happened and she had caused it. No-one would ever believe her, and she wouldn't blame them.

It might be easier to feign a confession. To say that she'd run away with Frank for a year …. Twice!

She was already imagining the consequences of it. The hatred and resentment and most of all, the rejection. No-one would want her back after a confession like that. A mother and wife who'd decided to make a new life twice and then returned when it didn't work out! A woman who'd run away again without even waiting for her daughter to return from a sleepover!

As she turned onto Station Road, she could already see the huge gates through which she would peer with Brenda. The gates that were occasionally open when the family were out, allowing them to spin around that circular drive and try to make out shapes behind the dimpled glass door.

It was no time for reminiscing.

In a few minutes that door would open, and she would be facing the shocked faces of Brian and Frankie! She needed a story to tell. A story that would somehow relinquish her from blame and prompt those arms into welcoming her back into the life she now, so desperately wanted.

There was only one story in the world that would suffice but she wasn't sure she had the energy or the will to try.

She had to feign the disorientation and confusion associated with a person who had suffered incredible memory loss. Who had no recollection of where she had been or how she had managed to return. No recollection of those missing years.

As she pulled open the heavy gate and made her way to that dimpled front door it didn't occur to her that her fabricated alibi was practically the truth.

Before knocking, Amelia retrieved the note from her pocket and read it again as though checking the facts before committing. Of no longer trusting that anything would remain the same for a few minutes at a time.

The note hadn't changed. The address was still waiting on that scrap of paper, the way it had waited for a whole year in handwriting she didn't even recognise.

She folded it carefully, almost lovingly and knocked.

She was already preparing herself for another disappointment when she heard muffled voices from inside. One voice seemed to be that of a woman but the other was definitely that of a child.

Her heart pounded.

She could already feel it.

Her family were right behind that front door. She felt the familiarity of them, the connection between them. Like some primeval instinct was at work. This was the home of her pack, her creed, her tribe!

She strained her eyes against the dancing colours of the mottled glass as a figure approached.

It was nothing more than an outline of colours as it reached for the handle, muttered, cursed and then moved away again.

Amelia sighed impatiently.

She hadn't recognised the outline, but it seemed to be that of a woman. A woman who had obviously misplaced the key.

The outline seemed too slender for Sheila but too heavy for Brenda. Perhaps it was Brian's mother or even a nannie! Whatever had happened that year it seemed that they'd come into some money!

The woman's voice was barely audible now. Somewhere at the back of the house but the child's voice was a little clearer.

Scenarios were already running through Amelia's mind.

Perhaps her father had sold the old house and pooled his money with Brian's parents to buy this place and share the childcare between the grandparents?

It was a warming thought.

The voices inside seemed to be approaching again but only the figure of the woman came into view. This time she came closer to the door as she fiddled with the keys and Amelia could see her more clearly.

She seemed to be an older woman of medium build with greying hair.

She opened the door a little and peered around it.

Suddenly, Amelia didn't know what to say.

She stood numbly on the step as one half of the woman's face waited in the silence.

It felt like a stand-off. Some kind of confrontation between them but still Amelia had no opening line to defuse it.

Then the door started to move. Slowly, the door was opening without a sound until the spectacled woman stood fully in the open doorway.

Amelia remained silent as the thin lips on that wrinkled face suddenly started to quiver.

"Amelia!"

It was no more than a whisper.

Amelia peered back at the woman who seemed to know her, but she didn't recognise the face or even the voice.

Suddenly the woman lurched forward and grabbed her around the shoulders.

"Mealy!"

Amelia couldn't breathe.

"Brenda?"

Chapter 3

Amelia closed her eyes slowly for protection.

Dropping a curtain between her fragile heart and the spectacle before her. Rejecting the images so desperately. This woman didn't sound or look like Brenda but as she hurled herself bodily at her paralysed visitor, throwing her arms around her, sobbing and whispering, Amelia could no longer deny the palpable recognition of the sweet soul emanating from that aged body.

These were the same arms that had clung to her a thousand times as a child.

This was little Bren.

"You're alive. You're alive." Brenda whispered into Amelia's neck. It was neither a question nor an exclamation. It was a whisper of thanks to God.

But Amelia was already sliding to the floor. Her body was giving up and, as she slid down the brick wall, she could feel the warmth of urine oozing down her legs.

As Brenda continued to whisper her gratitude and cling mercilessly to the miracle she'd given up on years ago, Amelia could do nothing other than to absorb the horrific truth.

This was not 1982!

As quickly as the nightmare had resonated, her desperate desire to thwart it took over.

More powerful than despair, her old enemy and tormentor returned.

Hope.

She stared up at that wilted face and summoned her voice.

"Oh God! Oh God! Brenda! What's happened?"

Brenda took her weight and tried to lift her back to her feet but her shaking legs refused to bear any weight and she started to collapse again.

Brenda practically carried her stunned, urine-soaked sister into the house, through to the living room and placed her gently in a chair.

"Where have you been Mealy?" Brenda whispered as she propped her against a cushion.

"I don't know." Amelia cried.

"I got out of bed this afternoon, while you were all talking in the kitchen, and I went up the lane to check on Frank. I spoke with him for a minute and then I went back home, and you'd all disappeared! Then some strange couple gave me this note which looks like it's been in a fuckin' museum and it brought me here! That's it! That's all I know."

Brenda's gentle face seemed to melt further.

Brenda knew her sister well. Even now. Amelia was telling the truth as she knew it to be!

"But Mealy, that was years ago. Decades ago."

She watched Amelia's eyes search her own for clarity and then they closed, and her mouth opened and from that mouth came a deafening scream.

Amelia screamed and screamed as Brenda held her tight and started to rock her back and forth.

Somewhere in the house a door slammed, and loud music started to blare but Amelia was incapable of hearing it.

The screams of hysteria continued for several minutes, abated for a few seconds, only to re-commence. Weak arms flailing pathetically at the air, as though trying to protect herself from some invisible attacker as Brenda fought to capture and hold them tightly as she shushed and rocked her beloved sister until she collapsed back into her arms with exhaustion.

The music quietened and Brenda lifted her onto the sofa, covered her with a throw and settled on the floor beside her to keep vigil.

Shockingly, the sight of Amelia's youthful face failed to alarm her because this is how she'd imagined the miracle of her sister's return to unfold. This was the face she remembered. The only face she remembered. Never, in the passing years had she imagined an older version of her absent sister. This was just Mealy returning exactly as she'd left. Exactly as Brenda imagined her to look. Still wearing that old coat she'd snatched from the hook. The coat that felt cold and wet and still smelled damp despite the warm dry afternoon.

When Amelia opened her eyes again, the image of her sister's face brought with it the terrible realisation that she was not waking from some horrific nightmare.

The house was still unfamiliar, and her sister was still old and greying.

She tried to smile but her brain seemed incapable of instructing her body to do anything at all.

"Oh Mealy." Brenda stroked her hair and with each tender stroke Amelia felt her spirit starting to return. The logical, resilient scientist inside was urging her to take control and fix this. The words of her former self echoed through her aching head. "Before you can solve or cure something, first you need to understand it."

"I need a pen and paper!" She said suddenly.

Brenda stood back.

"What!"

"Please Bren. Do you have a pen and paper?"

Instinctively, Brenda reacted in the way she always had, and scuttled off to obey her big sister.

In the background a radio was still quietly playing. A tuneless chant of spoken angry words that Brenda would call rap and Amelia would never recognise as music at all.

As she waited for the coveted pen and paper, she failed to question the child's voice she'd heard from the doorstep.

She was focussed only on her task to reverse whatever had happened to her. Hope was her only focus now.

She had been dealt a problem and she was going to tackle it in the only way she knew how. She was going to use the gift she'd been given. Her intelligence. Her logic. If there was a chance that whatever had been done could be undone, she was going to find it!

With the swiftness of optimism, she grabbed the notebook and pen from Brenda's outstretched hand.

"I'll make some tea." Brenda said quietly.

She took out two cups and filled the kettle without once taking her eyes from her sister. Terrified that if she didn't keep her within sight, she might evaporate again. This time, never to return.

Amelia was scribbling frantically in her heavy, damp coat.

Dates and times. Minutes and hours.

Never once did Brenda challenge her or accuse her of anything. This was her Mealy and she trusted her implicitly. Just as she always had. They were in this together.

As the tea was quietly rested on the table Amelia looked up.

"I think I know what happened!" Amelia whispered. As though a greater power might be listening to her plan and thwart any effort she made, to negate the joke it had played on her.

Brenda sat down as Amelia turned the paper towards her.

"When I went to town this morning," she said eagerly.

Brenda flinched.

Amelia flinched in response.

In those few words, the colossal disparity of their grasp on the situation had been unleashed.

Amelia was still floundering around in the memories and mayhem of a Saturday long ago, but Brenda had lived a lifetime since that ancient, faded memory.

"What I mean is," Amelia quickly regained her stride. She wasn't going to allow the discrepancy to interrupt her theory. "when I got back with the milk, I kept saying that I'd been gone ten minutes didn't I?"

Brenda was still recovering from the revelation that Amelia believed the occurrence had only happened this morning and nodded numbly.

"but that doesn't mean I was with Frank for ten minutes because I'd spent about five minutes on the journey there and back."

"I don't know what you're trying to prove Mealy. Nothing is going to change." Brenda looked again at her sister's face. If this was an act, then she was playing the part well.

"It might do," she said firmly.

Brenda recognised this excitement. It was the same enthusiastic babbling she'd once inflicted on her when she'd desperately tried to show Brenda how she'd solved a gruelling equation.

Brenda had no more ability to either understand it or to recognise any value in it than she'd had when they were children.

"That means," Amelia continued as she pointed at her scribbling, "that approximately, five minutes equated to a year."

"So?"

"Well, I was worried that returning to Frank again might lose me another year, but I didn't consider the relationship of time."

"Were you?"

"Was I what?"

"Were you worried about it happening again?"

Amelia's face turned red.

Brenda had turned her theory into culpability. The confession of returning to Frank with the knowledge of the risk she was taking. Of the disregard for those who loved her.

Brenda watched her sisters face wilt.

The animated determination to solve the problem had been nothing other than a quest to relieve her insufferable remorse.

She felt that the confession was coming. Amelia was about to admit that she'd spent years hunting for Frank. That she probably had a whole new life somewhere and was now trying to masquerade as a woman with no memory of it all.

"You can tell me what really happened." She assured as she put her hand on Amelia's.

Amelia glared at her accusingly, causing her to mellow and smile. This was no time to challenge her.

"Go on." She said softly as she read the numbers Amelia had scribbled down "So every hour equates to twelve years?"

Amelia was both startled and relieved at her sister's yielding.

Brenda smiled and peered again over her shoulder at the numbers on the page.

Amelia's fortitude had mellowed. Her sister had somehow forgiven her for putting her passion for Frank before everything else. Before Brian and Frankie, dad and Sheila, and also before the love of the best friend she would ever have. Little Bren.

"Twelve years or there abouts, yes."

Amelia took a breath to sweep her guilt aside and continue.

"When I went back to check if Frank was still waiting, I'd been at home for most of the afternoon hadn't I?"

Brenda simply nodded.

"But when he saw me, he asked if I'd forgotten something. He said I'd hardly had time to go out of sight before I was back again! I should have realised that something was wrong right then. That something weird was going on with the timing of it."

"Maybe so, but it's too late now, Mealy."

"I just didn't see it! I'm an idiot! I then sat with him for a while, and he was so- so tired. I started to feel tired too. I should have jumped right out of that car and run for my life, but I rested my head on him."

Brenda watched the tears of regret and desolation start to pool in her lower lids.

"I opened my eyes and checked his watch, and it was just four o'clock. I hadn't left the house to meet him until just before that, so I thought everything was alright." The tears were starting to spill onto her cheeks. "but, if he thought I'd been gone for no time at all then it would still have been around one when I got in that car! In his time, it was still one o'clock! Then I checked his watch, and it was four o'clock. Bren, I think we fell asleep for about three hours. Three hours in that unearthly place of fucked-up time!"

"Thirty-seven years." Brenda said curtly.

"Thirty-six!" Amelia corrected.

"I wasn't doing the calculation Mealy, I was telling you how many years you've been gone. This is 2018"

Amelia looked blankly into her sister's weathered face and watched any hope of redemption slip away.

"I don't think I can fix this Bren."

"I know."

Brenda removed the pen and paper to reinforce the message.

"I didn't know what to think, Mealy." She sighed. "The police came here looking for Frank. He never made it on his flight back to Australia, but his hire car was back at the airport. Left at the car-hire drop off."

Amelia frowned.

"How did it get back there? Frank was in no state to drive."

Brenda ignored the question.

"What did they think had happened then?"

It was an easier question to answer without lying.

"Seems there were people after his blood, but I guess he told you that." She continued without waiting for confirmation. "For a long time, they thought that someone got to him at the airport or that the two of you left the car there as a decoy and ran off together under new names. To be honest, that's what I thought you'd done for quite a long time. Started a new life without us."

"What! Without Frankie! I would never leave Frankie!"

"It's just how it looked at the time."

"What changed?"

"What do you mean?"

"You said, that's what everybody believed for a long time so what changed? Did they find out what really happened to Frank?"

Brenda walked into the kitchen to fill the kettle.

She didn't need more tea, but she needed to hide her face.

She flicked on the kettle with unimaginable dread.

Her devastated guilt-ridden sister was barely holding things together and she hadn't yet been exposed to the full horror of those shocking years.

Why she'd ever continued to hope for Amelia's return was now beyond her.

No-one would want to inflict those terrible truths on someone they love.

This morning she had woken up with her usual sinking feeling. That familiar blend of dread and sorrow, but at least it had been no worse than any other day.

But now, as she flicked the kettle on and rinsed out the cups, she harboured an inconceivable wish.

She wished Amelia had never been given the note she'd left with the half-wits at their old house.

Had never witnessed the effort she'd put into buying their childhood dream house.

She wished she could protect her sister from what was to come.

She wished Amelia was dead.

Chapter 4

Amelia's frantic need to solve the mystery of her disappearance was slowly replaced by another. The need to know the whereabouts and well-being of her family.

"Do Brian and Frankie live here too?" She gushed. "Or is Frankie married? Do I have grandchildren? Where's dad and Sheila?

"Just give me a minute, Mealy." She replied softly as she handed over the cup of steaming tea and walked towards the door to the hallway.

Amelia took the cup and cradled it in her hands. It felt strangely comforting.

She took a sip.

"I'll just be a moment." Brenda smiled as she slipped out and closed the heavy oak door firmly behind her.

It was the first time Amelia had given any thought to the prospect that someone else was in that house.

She stared into the warm brown liquid and vaguely recalled a sudden booming of music amidst her own screaming, but it was all so vague.

Beyond that heavy door, Brenda crossed the hallway and pushed open another door. The door to the downstairs bedroom she'd kitted out after Sheila's last hip replacement.

As she entered the room Sheila's anxious eyes met hers as the ringleted little girl on her knee smiled widely and ran towards her.

Brenda caught the girl in her embrace but her attention remained on the old woman in the chair.

"Sheila! You'll never guess what's happened."

"I turned the music up so Gilly could dance, didn't I Gilly?" Sheila smiled.

"I wish you wouldn't call her that. It's Olivia not Gilly!"

Brenda instantly knew that Sheila had tried to drown out the screaming to protect Olivia from hearing it.

"Can we play snakes and ladders for money again?" Olivia asked. Already pulling the box from a stack in the corner.

"I'm going to be blamed for turning you into an under-age gambler!" Sheila replied as she tried to sit up straighter in her chair by digging her walking stick into the carpet.

As Olivia opened the box on the small table and unfolded the board, the two women exchanged another searching glance.

Brenda's eyes were as wide as saucers.

"Is this what I think it is?" Sheila asked, as casually as she could manage.

"Let me put it this way." Brenda glanced again at Olivia. "The prodigal daughter has just returned."

Sheila's face drained to a sickly grey.

"Are you sure!" She hissed.

Brenda simply nodded before heading back towards the door. She put her hand on the door handle and then glanced back.

"I can't get my head around it. I feel like I'm in a dream."

Sheila didn't reply. She was trying to balance her reaction to the incredible news with her resolution to act normally for Olivia's sake and the result was an emotionless gaze.

Brenda remained in the doorway. Reluctant to leave the comfort of Sheila's wisdom.

"Why now, Sheila? If there's a God out there somewhere then why now? When it's all too late!"

Sheila tried to refocus her stare and then turned her forlorn face back in Brenda's direction.

"Maybe it's not too late in his eyes, love. Maybe it's just in time?"

Brenda allowed Sheila's words to go unchallenged. Either way it seemed like a damn coincidence!

"I need you to play with Olivia for a while so I can talk to Mealy some more."

"Of course. Of course!" Sheila snapped. "Go. Go!"

"What does prog-gigal mean, Granny." Olivia asked as she retrieved Sheila's purse from the nightstand.

"It's someone who comes back from a long trip." Sheila explained as she opened her purse and started to share out the loose change between the two competitors.

"Like when mummy comes back home?"

Sheila felt the ache in her heart again.

"We'll see love. We'll see."

Brenda went upstairs to retrieve the envelope she'd been tempted to open a million times but never dared. She re-entered the kitchen with no idea of how she was ever going to answer Amelia's questions or to deal with the fallout.

She took her own cup and held it exactly as her sister was holding hers. Nestled between both hands. The way they would sit together by the fire at night cradling a mug of Ovaltine.

"Mealy. I don't know where to start."

"Just tell me. Tell me everything."

"I can't" Brenda started to cry. "It's all such a mess."

Amelia put her cup back on the table and cupped her sister's sobbing face with her teenage hands.

"Whatever it is, it can't be as devastating as losing thirty-seven years of your life Bren. It really can't."

Brenda looked up.

She fixed her eyes on Amelia's and immediately Amelia felt the dread of what was yet to come. Those eyes that used to be full of mischievous joy were now as cold as steel. Dead, lifeless eyes behind which the terrible truths were hidden.

Amelia shuddered.

This was bad. Very bad.

"Bren?"

Brenda decided to start at the beginning. For Amelia, the beginning had to be the day she'd walked back out of that door to find Frank but how could she tell her sister the whole story without giving away the secret she so desperately needed to keep?

On the day Amelia had gone missing from that bed had been the same day she'd opened the door to a man she barely recognised.

"Dad. You look terrible." She'd gasped as her father arrived after his long trip from Scotland.

Tom had instantly thrown his arms around her causing her to cry with relief. For a few moments she felt optimistic that the family could be repaired. That her affair with Brian might never reach her sister's ears and somehow, she would be forgiven.

"Where is she?"

"We left her to get some sleep.

Brenda's brief moment of optimism was soon to be totally annihilated.

Firstly, by the empty bed where Amelia had lain a few hours earlier then by the frustrated outburst from her father that he literally didn't have time for this.

This had been his last chance to see his family. Time was running out and the stupid girl had gone missing again!

There was no point in returning to Scotland now. He needed to stay close by in case she reappeared, and the Scottish air could no longer sustain him with any more success than the doctors who'd shook their heads apologetically and urged him to get his affairs in order.

It was all too late.

Tom Simpson spent his final months fading away in the house that had been their family home. Watching and listening for Amelia's reappearance as the clock ticked away his hope of ever setting eyes on her again. Haunted by the memories he'd tried to escape. Nursed by the forgiven daughter he now cherished.

He passed away in the house he'd shared with Celia without ever holding Amelia in his arms again.

"Bren?"

Brenda shook herself free of the memory of it.

"Dad was really sick, Mealy. He had a disease called asbestosis. He passed away a few months after you left again. He left us the house and an insurance pay-out. He said he'd learned the value of life insurance by being left to bring us up alone after mum died."

She felt Amelia's pain as powerfully as though it were her own and she couldn't bear to make it worse with any of the detail, so she simply handed over an envelope.

"He left you a letter."

As Amelia fumbled with the envelope, she heard a distant tune from somewhere else in the house.

Brenda was walking back towards the sink when suddenly the tune stopped, and Brenda started to talk to some imaginary person.! She remembered the man in the street doing the same thing. Some sort of madness seemed to be in play!

"Who are you talking to?" Amelia snapped as she scanned the room for the answer.

Brenda turned around and frowned. In her hand she held a small object.

"It's some bloody cold-caller."

Amelia had no idea what her sister was doing or saying. She might as well have been speaking another language.

The confused look on Amelia's face caused her to frown suspiciously.

"Of course. You haven't seen a mobile before, have you?"

"A mobile what?"

The only mobile Amelia knew of was a cot mobile!

"It's just a telephone."

She pressed a button on it before handing it over.

Amelia took the tiny object, turning it over and over before handing it back with a sigh.

"Nothing is the same." She sobbed, "I walked down our old street earlier. It was packed full of cars. What's happened Bren? I can't take any more."

Brenda walked over and stroked her sister's hair from her face. It felt exactly as it had when she used to plait it for her before bed. The same texture, length, and colour.

"Everyone has cars around here now" she said gently as she continued to rake the familiar hair through her fingers. "and not just one car but two or even three in a family. Our old street had no driveways or garages so they simply ram them everywhere they can get them. It's not a good look, is it?"

Amelia shook her head. Not just in agreement but in despair. The street that had once been their beloved playground was now a haphazard carpark.

As Brenda continued to soothe her with the gentle strokes, she opened the letter and Brenda read it over her shoulder.

'My dearest Amelia,

I am writing this while I still have the ability to hold a pen as my strength is diminishing at a startling rate. I returned from Scotland when I heard the news, but you had already disappeared again. I wanted so much to hold you one last time but I'm sure you had your reasons.'

Brenda was sure she'd felt Amelia's heart sink with guilt as she read that line.

'Everyone here seems to think you will return after a year again, but I won't make it that far, so I wanted you to know that I take all our memories with me.

You and I, we always had something special between us.'

Brenda felt her own heart sink this time. Amelia had always been dad's favourite.

Amelia turned the note over.

'I remember the nights we spent on your maths homework. I remember the one equation we never solved about Mrs Brown's blackout curtains (I kept it for years and I've written the answer below) Better late than never, eh?

I love you, Amelia. I don't know where you are or why but sometimes, I imagine that you're somewhere else entirely. Maybe with mum. If you are then I'll see you very soon love, but if you're reading this letter, then that means I've passed over and you're still here so you can tell me everything when you get there.

Be strong darling and don't be too hard on Brenda. Dad.'

Amelia folded the note carefully and returned it to the envelope without noticing Brenda's unease at the final sentence.

"He left us both the house and insurance?"

"Yes, he did. Well, that was until…"

"Until what?"

"Until you were declared dead, Mealy."

"I was declared dead!"

There was a short silence before Brenda grabbed her bodily and pulled her close. Instantly their bodies collapsed into heart-wrenching sobs.

Amelia was the first to break the stranglehold.

"I need a plan." She said firmly. "I need some goddamn stability. I need to know everything! Everything!"

Brenda nodded, keeping her misgivings to herself.

"I can't tell you everything Mealy. It's too awful but I just spoke to Sheila."

"Sheila's alive?"

"Yes, she is. She lives here. She's just over the hallway in her room. I think she's a better person to talk to than I am."

Amelia felt the instantaneous relief. The one person in the world who could help her to make sense of this. Her one glimmer of hope.

"Come on." Brenda puller her to her feet and led her over the hallway and into Sheil's bedroom.

As they entered, a small girl had just thrown a dice across the carpet.

Amelia glanced at the old woman in the chair beside the bed. She was clearly in her eighties, but that face was unmistakable and the twinkle in her eyes told Amelia everything she needed to know. This was her Sheila and nothing between them had changed.

The child looked up. Amelia smiled in her direction and a tentative half-smile was returned.

She wondered if the child was a relative of Sheila's or maybe even a relative of her own. A heart-shaped urchin face framed with a mass of tight brown ringlets. There was no family resemblance she could see.

"Come on Olivia." Brenda called cheerily. "Let's go and make supper. It's almost bedtime and Granny Sheila has a friend she needs to talk to."

The little girl stood up obediently, retrieved the dice and placed it in Sheila's hand. She then kissed Sheila on the cheek and took Brenda's extended hand.

"You go up and get your pyjamas on. I'll be there in a minute."

She listened to the footsteps making their way upstairs and turned back into the room.

"Amelia is trying to get us to believe that she fell asleep for a few hours and thirty-seven years slipped by!" She scoffed.

Amelia's face reflected the unexpected betrayal.

"You don't believe me." She mused quietly. "My own sister. My little Bren doesn't believe me. Have you any idea what I'm feeling right now!"

Brenda backed towards the door as Amelia turned to take her on.

"This morning I went out for a pint of milk and ten minutes later a whole year had gone by. Then…then this afternoon I went back to say goodbye to Frank so I could come back to my life with a clear conscience and guess what! My whole fuckin' life had disappeared!"

The two women were staring at each other without speaking when Sheila intervened. Just as she always had. The voice of reason.

"Brenda. Look at her. Come here and look at her."

Brenda moved closer.

"Do you see the same wrinkles on her neck that you have on yours? The same spider lines from her eyes? Do you?"

Before Brenda could respond she took the old, wrinkled, veined hand of Brenda's and matched it to the pink young hand of Amelia."

The shock on Brenda's face was instantaneous. She hadn't even noticed. Amelia was just Amelia. Returning exactly as she'd left. Exactly as Brenda had always imagined it.

Her eyes searched Sheila's for reassurance and then she allowed her nobbled fingers to curl around that pink young hand.

"I'm so sorry Mealy." She whispered as she kissed her on the cheek.

She felt Amelia's body relax with sheer submission and left her in the redeeming hands of their Sheila, before climbing the stairs with legs she could no longer feel and a heart she wished she couldn't feel.

Alone in that room, Sheila's eyes met Amelia's.

The air was suddenly dense.

Dense, heavy, and thick with emotion.

A silence charged with a lifetime of questions.

Amelia stood numbly, wating for Sheila to guide her, just as she always had. Sheila always knew what to do and and in that moment of uncertainty she needed more than ever before, for Sheila to take the lead.

The guiding star came in the form of a radiant smile and two outstretched arms.

Amelia didn't hesitate in rushing to fill them.

They folded around her like a huge warm blanket and the comfort was palpable.

"I've got you." Sheila whispered. "I've got you now."

This was a moment that needed no words.

It was unmistakably the blessed reunion of a mother and daughter.

Chapter 5

Upstairs, as Brenda finished the storybook and kissed Olivia goodnight, her stomach was churning.

It had been almost an hour since she'd left Amelia in Sheila's room, and no-one had yet emerged.

She could only imagine the pain her sister was suffering as the tragedies and heartbreak would be falling, one after the other, from Sheila's lips.

She crawled in beside Olivia for comfort and remained there with her own thoughts while the little girl slept.

She recalled the morning after Amelia disappeared that second time. The moment the front door burst open, and Frankie came running into the house.

"Mummy! Mummy! I'm here! It's me. Frankie!"

No-one had thought to call back the parents of Frankie's friend and tell them not to tell her that her mummy was back!

Amidst the trauma of Amelia's second disappearance and the shock of Tom's skeletal home-coming, the need to protect Frankie had slipped through the net.

Brian was the first to realise the consequence of their blunder as he scooped her into his arms and held her tight. "Mummy's not here right now princess but I'm sure she'll be back soon."

He felt Frankie sink in his arms. Her entire body seemed to drop with disappointment. It didn't matter what reassurance he would try to offer because the moment she'd been anticipating for the entire journey had been ruined. He held her in his arms until he felt her beginning to take her own weight again.

"Where did she go daddy?"

Brian wished he could answer his daughter's question. Wished he could give her some hope, but he couldn't.

Brenda remembered putting her arms around them and secretly hoping that Amelia would go back to her lover and leave them all alone to be a family again.

Over the next few days Brenda seemed to resent everything. She resented Brian's misplaced loyalty, their father's visible heartache, Sheila's optimism that Amelia would return again, and Frankie's relentless longing for her mother's love.

It was obvious that Amelia's selfish treachery had no impact on their collective longing to have her back. As little impact as her own sacrifices and hard work had on any collective gratitude for stepping into the breach.

This was all about Amelia. Just as it always had been, yet she still couldn't stop herself from praying just as avidly for her sister's safety and happiness.

There would be several moments when she almost blurted out the truth to Brian and to her dad. The urge to enlighten them about Amelia's confession of her plan to run away with Frank burned often in her heart, but the words that occasionally circled her mind, caged by loyalty, never found their way to her lips.

Her loyalty to Amelia would always be a little stronger than her loyalty to herself.

As the weeks turned to months the family gradually allowed hope to dissipate but Sheila refused to give up on her eldest surrogate daughter. She gently blew the embers of hope with the theory that Amelia would return the following year. That her story held some incredible, unlikely truth.

As summer ebbed away, yielding its warm sun-kissed days to the dreary grey coolness of autumn, Tom yielded to the debilitating final chapter of his life on palliative care.

Nursed at home by those who loved him, he spent his final weeks in the arms of Sheila. His first love who nursed him with every morsel of her being. Full of regret, of visions of what might have been, what could have been and what should have been. In his final days she saw her own heartache reflected back at her in his eyes. So many wasted years! His fear that he had made a huge mistake. That nothing existed beyond this life and as she watched him fade away, she prayed that Celia would be waiting for him. She prayed with all her heart, because if it wasn't so, then everything had been for nothing.

His breaths became less frequent, and she held his hand more tightly as though trying to anchor him to this world.

She closed her eyes and whispered to him.

"You can rest now, my love. Go find Celia."

She opened her eyes to find his also open again. He couldn't speak but he was telling her everything that he could in the tears that glistened and pooled their story of regret and remorse. His eyes were speaking to her in a way she once remembered from decades ago when they spoke of love and promises but today, they told spoke of a life stolen from them by his own stupidity. Of heartbreak and a plea for forgiveness.

She smiled her forgiveness and felt his hand curl around her fingers for just a second before it relaxed again and his fingers fell open.

Tom had left this world.

She lay with her head on the pillow beside him and held him in her arms for an entire hour before returning to Brenda to break the news.

Then, without explanation or apology, she returned to Barry to continue her relationship with the man who knew better than to challenge the ferocity of her vigil or to interfere with her grief in any way.

After the funeral, her attention turned back to another member of her adopted family. Amelia!

Neither Brenda nor Brian shared her theory of Amelia's annual return but, as winter turned to spring again, it brought with it a growing sense of awareness. The feeling that something momentous was drawing near. Without ever discussing or acknowledging the cause of it, the entire household was becoming agitated, restless, and underneath this disquiet ran an unmistakable hint of anticipation.

As March closed its door, the unrest grew into a sense of impending doom. The day of reckoning was approaching, and the calendar had turned into some huge silent clock which ticked and tocked each day away, in deafening silence to Monday 19th April 1982.

On Sunday night no-one slept except Frankie, who had no perception of the calendar or of any outrageous theories relating to her mother's disappearance.

Brenda had held Frankie in her arms for the entire night. Savouring the hours that might be her last moments of motherhood.

Brian stared up at the ceiling and wished for the whole thing to be over. He watched his alarm clock innocently ticking through the countdown until its familiar racket announced the arrival of the auspicious day. The day of the predicted second coming.

As it was a Monday, thankfully Frankie was bundled off to school while the rest of the family tried to pretend it was a normal day.

Brian went to work, Brenda did the washing and Sheila mowed Barry's lawns and re-arranged the gnomes, but all three members of the clan kept one eye on the door, the gates, and the streets.

Independently yet collectively, they were wating. Waiting and anticipating. Dreading and hoping. Consumed by the possibility that Amelia would turn up in her old damp coat and fall back into their arms.

But that night as Frankie was tucked up in bed something changed. Everything changed.

All flickers of hope were silently but firmly extinguished. Amelia was gone. Her fate unknown. The two possibilities would no longer be agonised over. She was either living her life with Frank and her story had been pure fabrication or she was dead. Extinguished with her lover in some revenge attack. Either way, she had chosen Frank over her family and for that they could at least lay the blame at her door and get on with their own lives.

They abandoned their collective considerations for Amelia and reverted back to the life they'd forged before her dramatic return.

Brenda moved back into the marital bed with Brian and Amelia's clothes were bagged up for the charity shop but this time there were two major differences.

Brenda didn't sneak out from that bed before Frankie woke up and suddenly, quite miraculously, Frankie started to call her mummy.

They had become a family even though most of the village jokingly referred to the newly joined couple as Beauty and the Beast.

But today, as she lay beside little Olivia, with Amelia only yards away downstairs, she sighed at the irony of it.

Brenda had longed to be a mother her entire life, but it just wasn't to be. For years she had tried to give Brian a baby of his own but Mother nature hadn't blessed her with that ability. She'd blessed her with great beauty but also with polycystic ovaries. She was the pretty one but not the fertile one.

She turned Olivia onto her side and slid out from the covers.

She needed to know what was going on with Sheila and how much her sister now knew.

She crept quietly down the stairs and pressed her ear against Sheila's door.

There was no screaming or sobbing.

Either Sheila hadn't told her very much or Amelia was held in the grip of despair.

She heard Sheila say something about mice in the attic and her heart skipped a beat.

This was it!

Sheila was about to tell her how their entire family fell apart!

She went into the kitchen and poured herself a large glass of wine before sitting down to wait for the explosion.

The day Sheila was talking about was in the autumn of 1985 when Frankie was ten.

Probably the happiest time of their lives until those damn mice destroyed it all.

The notion of a sibling for Frankie had been mourned and eventually accepted. Frankie and Brian were working hard on getting her a place in the top stream at secondary school. Brian had a way of making everything fun, including geometry and fractions. He would make little props to demonstrate, and Frankie would laugh at his animated antics to get the logic to stick.

Sometimes Brenda would watch proudly as her mismatched family flourished but sometimes her heart would ache that Amelia could not see the beauty of her daughter or the relationship that little girl had with Brian.

It was true that Amelia hadn't been particularly blessed in the beauty department but the combination of her genes with Frank's had more than compensated.

Frankie's strong black hair now hung to her waist and reminded Brenda of a Hawaiian hula girl or an Indian squaw. Her facial features were strong and beautiful, and her lips had a fullness that Amelia had not been blessed with. Her skin was olive like Franks, not blotchy and pale like Amelia's. Brenda knew how it felt to turn heads because she'd walked in those shoes. Been raised with the frequent comments from strangers of 'Isn't your daughter pretty!' yet, strangely, no-one ever called Frankie pretty. They always used the word beautiful. It was a subtle difference, but Brenda understood it completely.

It had been in those days of Frankie's transformation from chubby child to beautiful young girl that the axe fell.

For days they had heard the scurrying of mice in the attic.

"They've been driven from the fields during the harvest." Brian laughed. "They'll go back when the machine's leave."

"No they won't, they'll be settling up there for the winter and multiplying if we don't get rid of them!" Brenda had replied irritably. "Honesty Brian, you're far too soft!"

"I'll pick up some poison then." Brian laughed again. "But I'm not going to be the one who kills off Micky and Minnie!"

Brenda knew he was just appeasing her. There was no way Brian would buy poison to kill a defenceless animal, so she went to the hardware shop and bought it herself before marching to the shed in search of the ladder.

She broke her nail picking at the knotted nylon string that secured it to the shed roof and then wrestled the cantankerous lump of straggling metal up the stairs as it opened and closed onto her unsuspecting fingers. Angry and determined she eventually manoeuvred the clattering beast into a position where she could climb to open the hatch. After three huge, vertical shoulder charges she managed to crack open the nestled plank of wood that somehow always managed to reseal itself to the frame with paint residue.

She poked her head into the blackness and realised that she needed a torch. She'd been asking Brian to connect a light up there, but it was never going to get onto his priority list and the only torch they possessed had been left out in the rain a few weeks ago. She was going to have to return to the hardware shop to buy a torch and batteries. It felt like fate was determined to stand in her way and by the time she got back she'd almost given up and decided that Brian could do it himself since he'd made the whole task such a dicktat!

But then she made herself a mug of coffee and her determination got the better of her. She wasn't going to give him or fate the satisfaction of her failure!

Not once did she consider that fate might be on her side, fighting to protect her not the mice. Placing obstacles in the way of a lifechanging, devastating blow.

Within a minute she was back up the ladder with a battery-loaded torch in hand.

She held the torch under her arm and filled the empty margarine tub with poison before scanning around for a place to leave it.

She considered that it ought to be put under the insulation somewhere so no visiting sparrows would be accidentally poisoned instead.

She shone the torch over suitcases, rolls of wallpaper remnants, old schoolbooks, and Christmas decorations.

The Christmas decorations always made her smile that melancholy smile. They were the same decorations they'd had since her childhood. The same decorations she and Amelia had squabbled over as they hung each one on the tree. Then there had been the mystery of the large red bauble which had become a standing joke. It had been her mother's favourite. A huge glass bauble with a silver sleigh of glitter around it which had suddenly disappeared one year, never to return.

Celia had accused everyone in turn of breaking it and hiding the evidence, and although she had been upset on the first year of its disappearance it had quickly become a source of annual hilarity and relentless speculation.

She flashed the torch in that direction and decided that the poison would be safest in the place that was only disturbed once a year.

She peeled back the fluffy insulation and placed the tub carefully beneath it before turning to crawl back to the hatch.

But as she started to crawl away, she couldn't help thinking that her torch might have skimmed over a flash of something red and silver beneath the insulation.

By the time she reached the hatch she was pretty sure that it was nothing other than the light playing tricks but as she put one foot back on the ladder, she was getting that nagging feeling of wanting to go back and check.

She imagined how funny it would be to solve the mystery of the bauble after all these years even though there was no-one left to share it with!

She sat with her legs on the top rung of the ladder and allowed her heart to ache. Holding that illusive bauble again would be the most wonderful and terrible feeling she could imagine. All three of them would be vindicated but no-one but her, would ever know it.

She picked the torch up from the floor of the attic and headed back towards the decorations.

She sat for a moment with one hand on the corner of the wad of insulation before taking a deep breath, peeling it back and shining the torch into the void.

She gasped.

She'd been right that something red and silver had caught her eye, but it wasn't the missing bauble she was staring at.

It was Amelia's red overnight case!

The case she said she'd smuggled into Frank's car so many years ago.

The missing case that led the police to believe she'd run away.

She dragged it towards her and flipped the catch.

Inside was a few neatly packed clothes of Amelia's and Frankie's and in the lid was her passport.

Her heart was pounding as her brain span like a roulette wheel, with the ball bouncing from slot to slot, each rejected until it settled into the only slot that made any sense. The only explanation her brain hadn't rejected.

Her pounding heart became still and lifeless as it soaked in the seeping dread.

There was only one other person who ever went into that loft!

Chapter 6

That was the day everything changed.

The day everything fell apart.

The dreadful day that Sheila was now divulging to Amelia as Brenda gulped down the rest of the wine in the kitchen.

Amelia would probably already know by now about her relationship with Brian. About the way she'd stolen her sister's man and adopted her sister's life as her own. In a few more minutes Amelia would learn of another betrayal. A betrayal that would break her heart.

After dragging the case from the loft and stashing it in her wardrobe, Brenda had tried to act normally until the moment Frankie was asleep in bed.

She then opened the wardrobe, pulled out the case and placed it on the bed in which Brian was sitting.

He stared at the offending object and then at the beautiful but terrified eyes of his lover. He could feel her desperation as she raked her blonde tresses back through her fingers nervously. She was aching for him to relieve her of the anguish of that most obvious explanation. Aching for the reassurance that would allow her to continue to live this life she'd grown to love. Something, anything, that would prove he'd had nothing to do with her sister's disappearance!

Seconds ticked by. Seconds that should have been filled with his innocent bewilderment or believable explanation, but those seconds remained barren. Empty yet full. Silent but screaming.

His frantic story of vindication never materialised. His cobbled string of excuses or plausible explanation failed to emerge.

She should have expected nothing less from Brian.

He wasn't a crafty, devious player. Not a shrewd, sneaky cunning man.

Scheming, lying, and deception were not a part of his makeup. It was why she loved him so much but today she wished with all her heart that he would dig deep for a believable lie.

The face before her on that day was simply the face of submission. The face of a little boy who would take whatever punishment he deserved but as she allowed that silence to paint the picture, she needed to know one thing.

"Brian. Have you done something to my sister? To Amelia?"

His face turned instantly from desolation to raging disbelief.

"Of course not! How could you think that!"

"Well, somehow you managed to get her case back and I know for a fact that she gave that case to Frank."

"How do you know that?"

"She told Sheila that day. When she came back with the milk and the ridiculous story about being gone for ten minutes. She was leaving you and taking Frankie with her, but I think you knew that didn't you?"

Brian didn't respond.

"You must have seen Frank. Seen both of them! Why was her case hidden in the loft Brian? What did you do!"

Brian had neither the strength nor the willpower to put up a defence. She could tell from his body language that he was totally defeated. He wasn't going to fight to save himself or to save the life they had. The family they'd built.

"I didn't mean to hurt anyone."

Brenda's heart was pounding again.

"What did you do?" She repeated.

He looked right into her eyes and saw the dogged desperation to salvage whatever could be salvaged. It gave him the courage to speak because it had given him hope.

Brenda would try to understand. Try to stand by him. She would fight to protect her family even if he didn't have the resolve to.

"Yes, I knew what she was planning to do. I could read her like a book. I could feel her scheming plans as strongly as if she'd told me herself."

Brenda frowned but she knew exactly what Brian was telling her.

"Oh my God. You used to watch them doing that 'tuning in' thing didn't you? The thing I did with her before he came along? She used to say that you were always asking about it. Following them. She thought you were just lonely, but you were trying to learn how to do it!"

"Guess so but I wasn't very good at it, but I learned how to sense when she was up to something. Mostly when we were laying in bed quietly. I could feel her deceit."

"So why didn't you confront her?"

"I didn't want to ruin everything. I just wanted to ruin her plan to leave us. To get Frank to leave us alone. I knew he was back. I could feel the excitement in her."

Brenda sat down on the bed beside him.

Just as he had felt the presence of Frank in their lives, he could feel the love and resilience of Brenda. She didn't want to lose her family either.

"I saw her the day she met him to hand over her case."

"You followed her?"

He nodded.

"I watched her. She smiled at him and then she got in the car. They went to a hotel, and I waited in the carpark for hours torturing myself with every love scene I could imagine. Then I went back to work."

He propped himself against a pillow to continue his story. He seemed both relieved and almost proud to be sharing it.

"She made up some story about a Tupperware party at the community centre, but I checked and there was nothing on that day, so I left work early and took them both in the car."

"Why?"

"I wanted to see if she would choose him over me. I wanted to put her in that position. To face the reality of dragging Frankie away from the life she knew. I wanted us all together in that car so she could see what she was giving up and it worked. His car was right there. I saw her peer down the dirt track and I knew he was waiting for them. I invited her to get out at the lights, but she didn't. It was a relief and a victory. I really felt that she was mine again."

"Then what?"

"Then I saw the look on her face as I dropped them off in town. She wasn't a woman who'd just chosen her family. Nor a woman relieved and contented at having done the right thing. She was a woman distraught with regret. Frantic with remorse. A woman desperate to get back to the man who'd spent that afternoon in bed with her. Desperate to feel the weight of his perfect body on top of her again!"

Brenda didn't dare to speak. She could feel his jealousy burning through his core.

"I dropped them off then I drove back to the lane to warn him off. He used to be my friend at one time, and I wanted to beg him to leave us alone."

"He didn't listen?"

Brian looked at her. She felt the chill of it.

"By the time I got back there I was so bloody frustrated and angry and determined. I just wanted him gone. I wanted him to be in no doubt that I was going to fight with everything I had to keep her."

Brenda felt the chill again.

"I got out of the van and picked up a wrench. I just wanted him to feel threatened. I never intended to use it, honestly, I didn't. The rain was still lashing down and the lane was dark and muddy but as I approached, he was looking down at something and didn't even notice me approaching. It all happened so quickly. The change of plan I mean. I walked right by him, opened the back door and hit him at the back of the head. It was a moment of madness. Desperate uncontrollable madness. Then that was it."

Brenda felt the blood drain away until she became an empty shell who could no longer move any part of her body. Brian didn't seem to notice the impact of his words as he continued.

"He flopped onto the wheel and his eyes were just fixed in his head. I knew right away that he was dead. I remember seeing the printed paper on his lap that he'd been looking at. It was the flight details. Booking in times. He must have been trying to calculate if they still had time. I kind of felt a bit sorry for him."

Brenda was now so lightheaded that she could barely absorb the words that continued to bombard her.

She couldn't speak but she didn't need to because Brian seemed hell-bent on taking his horrific confession to its conclusion.

"Then I panicked. I knew Amelia would be heading back to that lane as soon as she could, so I had to get rid of it. Of all of it."

His words grew more frantic as he described his state of mind at the time.

"I dragged him from the car into the ditch and covered him in undergrowth then I drove the car a few streets away and returned for my van and went to see Barry. I got him to drive the hire car back to Manchester for me."

"Barry knew about this!"

"No. Of course he didn't. I just told him I needed a favour. He owed me one."

Brenda's head was reeling.

"He must have asked questions?"

Brian took a breath and sighed.

"He knew it was something to do with keeping Frank and Amelia apart but that was all. I did the same for him when I persuaded your dad to go to Scotland and leave the path clear for him and Sheila."

Brenda was simply watching the face of the man she'd built a life with and wondering if she ever knew him at all. His lips continued to move but the words were now out of the reach of her ears or mind.

This was the face that had held a thousand secrets behind those lips. This was the face of a murderer.

She needed to be careful what she said next and how she reacted as she refocussed on what he was telling her.

"I went back to my garage for a spade and parked at the other side of the roadworks. From there I could slip into the trees and get back to the track without being seen from the road. I dug a hole in the bottom of the ditch and rolled him in. Then I buried him, covered the area in undergrowth again and came back to wait for Amelia and Frankie to return."

Brenda knew the story from there.

That was when her sister decided they desperately needed milk and disappeared for an entire year.

As she sat numbly processing the revelation, she caught a glimpse of Brian's face out of the corner of her eye.

A forlorn, remorseful, pitiful face.

It wasn't the face of a murderer at all.

It was the face of a man who had so desperately fought to keep the family he loved. The wife he adored and the little girl he worshipped.

She felt the involuntary smile break onto her face.

She watched Brian's whole body relax.

"I didn't want to hurt anyone." Brian sobbed.

"I know you didn't."

"You don't hate me?"

"I don't hate you."

She got into bed beside him and held him in her arms.

That night they made love with a strange intensity. An alliance had been formed between them and it had been signed and sealed as they rocked each other to the brink of that inevitable climax.

Then they shuddered their treacherous treaty and fell apart to sleep.

An hour later, Brenda was awake again. Propped on one elbow with her flaxen hair draped beside Brian's face, she was studying him again. Wishing she could see inside. Know his thoughts the way she used to know Amelia's.

She could forgive his act of desperate passion. She could understand it but as she lay beside him, she started to wonder if he'd done something else. Something she could never forgive!

One thing was certain. Something incredulous had happened that day. Amelia was convinced she'd spoken to Frank in that car. Spoken with the man who had already been buried. Spoken in the car that had already been moved! She felt suddenly nauseous, and her body started to shake.

She needed to get out of bed and remove herself from the situation as best she could.

She needed space away from Brian to think. To consider his explanation.

He'd admitted to killing Frank but now she was wondering what really happened afterwards.

Amelia would have returned on the bus and dropped Frankie off to go back and find him.

Perhaps Brian had known she wasn't going out for milk but to return to Frank. The man she really wanted.

She tried to recall any private conversation between Amelia and Brian a year later, on that day she returned with the milk.

They were all in the kitchen when Amelia sneaked out again but perhaps there had been an argument between her and Brian. An argument about where she'd been and why she hadn't managed to track down Frank!

The bed had been empty, by the time her father arrived from Scotland, but she couldn't remember if Brian had been in the house for the entire time or if he could have heard her leave and followed her. No-one had set eyes on her sister since!

She banged her head with the heel of her hand to shake the memories loose, but she just couldn't remember.

Could he have confessed what he'd done to Amelia? Had she left that bed to go to the Police and report Frank's murder? Had Brian gone after her to shut her up!

Amelia would have been outraged, uncontrollable.

She sat alone for an hour trying to piece it all together. Amelia's imagined ten minutes with a dead man. Brian's burning desire to salvage his family. Her own loyalty to Brian and to her sister.

Eventually she climbed the stairs and laid back down beside Brian. Her arm crept around him. Gentle, moral, sweet, devoted Brian and this time, she slept.

In the morning she made breakfast and kissed Brian fondly as he left for work.

Frankie was about to leave for school when Brenda pulled her back for the kiss that she squirmed from every day.

"I'm too old for all that!" Frankie snapped with a half-smile.

Brenda then put on her coat and walked down the street to the police station.

"Can I help you?" The young male officer asked politely.

"Yes." Brenda replied firmly as she placed the red case on the counter. "I would like to report a double murder."

Chapter 7

Brian's arrest came swiftly.

He was taken in for questioning from the garage later that morning and never returned to that house again.

Many times, Brenda would recall that last kiss as she ushered him off to work. Many times, she would feel the weight of regret and of the dread that she might have made an enormous mistake. She hadn't really cared what he'd done to get rid of his rival, but she did care that he had most likely killed her sister in some jealous rage.

The uncertainty became her constant companion. Mocking and tormenting her as she swayed back and forth between the two compelling facts. Brian would never hurt Amelia was something of which she felt certain but Amelia's sudden disappearance on the same day she'd returned back to her family was too big a co-incidence. She'd been so desperate to see Frankie and her father again, yet something had caused her to go out again. The only explanations she could think of was a threat from Brian however unlikely that felt, or to report the murder of her lover by her husband.

Her only comfort was that she had done the moral thing. It was not her place to decide guilt or innocence to serve her own purpose. It was up to the police and the jury to unravel the truth of it.

How wrong she had been to ever take any comfort in that.

If she'd known the impact her actions were to have on Frankie, she would have taken that case back into the loft and buried it along with her misguided morals in a heartbeat.

Nothing. Not even the avenging of her sister's murder was worth the damage to her beloved niece, her surrogate daughter. Amelia would never have paid that price. She would rather her death remain unsolved.

Brian's confession came as swiftly as his arrest.

The road into town was closed and littered with police and forensic vehicles as the search for Frank's body commenced.

Frankie was kept home from school to protect her from the gossipmongers, the speculation, and from the cruel teasing of classmates who vented their fear in the only way children knew how. In the safety and solidarity of collective name-calling.

Suddenly they were isolated.

Brenda and Frankie existed in a world of their own as days came and went with only the lifeline of Sheila to cling to.

Brenda had brought the weight of the world down upon them and now there was no going back.

Shockingly the one person she longed to cling to was now sitting in a remand cell. Never had her love for Brian been stronger and there was still a chance that she had thrown it away to get justice only for the floppy haired boy from school that she barely knew. Brian remained steadfast that he had never laid a finger on Amelia and with each passing day, Brenda's trust in him grew.

Then, just when it seemed that nothing could get any worse, Barry was arrested.

The news came amidst the frantic rantings from Sheila who'd bullied her way through the reporters at Brenda's gate before collapsing into an armchair.

It was Brenda's turn to step up. To be the strong one and support the woman who'd supported her for her entire life, but it wasn't easy.

Every word or act of comfort was tainted with the indisputable fact that she had been the cause of everything that had rained down on them.

She hadn't been the one to swing that wrench, but she was swinging it now and it was hitting every single person she cared about.

She had learned a brutal lesson.

The lesson that honesty is not always the best policy. That justice for one person is not worth the injustice to everyone else.

That sometimes, two wrongs do make a right.

Thankfully Barry was released without charge of conspiracy to commit murder, aiding and abetting, or of being an accessory after the fact.

He'd been released back into society as a naïve nincompoop who took a car back to Manchester without asking questions as a favour to a friend. It was obvious that Brian had played a huge part in his release and Sheila knew it. Barry would have asked questions. It was an unusual request, and he would have been interested.

"Barry would never have been involved in something like this." Brenda reassured as she poured Sheila a large glass of brandy.

"No. You're right." Sheila replied but her tone was sarcastic. "He didn't want to know. I've already grilled him and that was the crux of it. He didn't ask because he didn't want to know."

"Why not?"

"Because he knew Brian was up to something, that's why and this is the best bit." She leant forward to make sure Brenda would take it in. "He owed Brian a favour!"

"Who calls in a favour with something like this!" Brenda scoffed.

"Oh, it gets even better," she emptied the glass in one swig. "He'd got Brian to persuade your dad to go to Scotland. Out of the way you see. To keep him away from me!"

Brenda sighed.

"If that's true then he was only trying to keep you in his life. Barry loves you."

"Well, thanks to him, your father went through that entire bloody illness alone. Without me! I would have been there. I would have brought him home or moved to bloody Scotland to be by his side!"

Sheila started to cry.

She had never seen Sheila cry before, and it wrenched her heart.

Frankie gently pushed open the door but stood silently in the gap.

"Come here, Frankie." Brenda whispered as she held out an arm.

Frankie rushed over and clung to Brenda, causing her heart to break all over again.

"Next year you'll be at secondary school. We'll move a bit further away and get a new start. Everything will be alright."

"I don't want to move away." Frankie sobbed. "What if mummy comes back and we've all gone?"

As Frankie spoke those words it seemed like another weight had just been dropped on top of the unbearable burden Brenda was already trying to bear.

Every one of her mistakes and unforgiveable decisions had come home to roost.

Her early lust for a glamourous life with a string of older men and playboy cads. Stealing her sister's husband. Stealing her sister's life and her child. Stealing Brian's freedom. Ripping a loving father and daughter apart for the best of their years together, and now the biggest mistake of all…. infecting Frankie with her own futile, relentless hope that Amelia would one day, walk back through that door.

"I don't think it's likely that your mummy will come back now darling." She whispered to the top of Frankie's head.

She felt Frankie's body slump slightly before she stiffened and pulled away.

"I'm going to finish my homework." She announced as she pulled away with a fake smile.

Brenda allowed her to leave her arms unchallenged. It was a cowardly thing to do, and she was already regretting it as Frankie walked to the door but she didn't have the emotional capacity to do anything else, so she turned her attention back to the matter in hand.

"I expect Barry is in the doghouse then?"

"Doghouse? He's in worse than the doghouse! He's in his own bloody house and he can flipping-well rot there. My overnight case is in the hall. I'll go back for the rest of my stuff as soon as that rabble of bloodsuckers have gone from the gate."

"You're moving back in?"

"If you'll have me, of course. My own place is rented out 'til next year."

"Of course." Brenda's mood was instantly lifted by the news, but Sheila continued to rant.

"As if there wasn't enough drama in our family without Barry shovelling in his spade full! The man's a total fuckin' dickhead!"

Brenda laughed spontaneously.

She had never heard language like that from Sheila before and, for a moment, it managed to ignite a glimmer of humour in their damp dismal existence.

Frankie returned to her room and sobbed.

No-one seemed to notice that she had just been orphaned, and no matter how hard she tried to make her new mum into the mummy she'd lost, it was never going to be the same.

She would never say it out loud but calling her auntie Brenda mum, didn't really make it true.

The love and devotion she received was indisputable and she knew that her new mum was giving everything she possibly could to fill the hole her mummy had left in her life but there was one thing that couldn't be replaced. It had been years now but as she sat on her bed, she could still remember the touch of her mummy. There was no mistaking that feeling whether it was a kiss, a hug, or a hand around her own. It had the power to warm her from the inside out and she hadn't felt that from anyone since. The feeling of absolute safety and total reassurance.

Sometimes, she told herself that she was just imagining it but then there were times, just like this, when she sat alone, closed her eyes and remembered. The comfort of her mummy's touch flooded back. It felt like connecting to another part of herself. Like they were one person, sharing each other's thoughts and feelings, hopes, fears and dreams and she ached inside to feel that again. Even for one last time.

To hear that tuneless voice softly singing the words to Cilla Black's 'You are my World' and as she now sobbed into her pillow, she realised that the one word she hadn't understood in that song was probably the best description of that unique feeling. A divine power passing between two people life a force of nature that would never be paralleled.

When her chest ached, and her eyes were too sore to cry any more she splashed cold water on her face and waited for the redness to fade.

Her mum didn't deserve to be demoted to auntie Brenda because she loved her even if her touch wasn't like her mummy's used to be.

A few days later, the remainder of Sheila's ample belongings were delivered by a cordial, broken man.

Barry simply placed the bags and boxes in the hallway before nodding politely to Brenda and leaving.

It felt like the end of the world but, at least, Sheila was back.

Chapter 8

The public gallery was packed full for every day of Brian's trial. Strangers hungry for the drama of it and neighbours desperate for the gossip surrounding the platinum blonde mother with the raven-haired adopted daughter. Housewives from their own street queuing outside to be certain of getting a seat from which they could watch the mystery unfold. Feeding on their misery and taking scraps back to satisfy the hunger of their husbands and children when they returned home.

Brenda, Barry and Sheila were all called to give evidence, but Frankie escaped the ordeal, being no more than a small child when her mother and Frank disappeared.

Amazingly, despite the probing questions and trickery of both barristers no-one ever mentioned Amelia's disturbing claim about her missing year. Sheila, Brenda and Brian maintained that Amelia had been missing for a year before returning to the household for no more than a few hours before sneaking out again. Presumably having discovered the fate of her lover and causing Brian to panic and finish her off. It was a simple explanation and although Brian continued to deny causing any harm to Amelia, even he, protected Amelia's claim to having spent time with a dead man.

Neither Brenda nor Brian wanted to pour more fuel onto the blazing circus that had become Frankie's life. This single aim strangely bonded them as they closed ranks to protect their ten-year-old daughter from hearing of the insane rantings of her real mother.

Neither of them had played a part in her creation but still they stood together steadfastly as her parents.

Then, although Brenda had been the one to bring the murderer to justice, she also stepped up as his salvation.

She gave her evidence compassionately and reluctantly. being careful not to reveal her own intimacy with the abandoned father. To the jury, she had been nothing more than the aunt who returned to take care of Frankie when her sister ran away with another man.

"Brian is a good man." She told the twelve upright members of her hometown. "He loved my sister with all his heart and the prospect of losing her was just too much to bear at that moment I think."

"So, you think your sister got what she deserved?" The barrister asked haughtily.

"No! No, she didn't because I know my sister is still alive. He might have gone after Frank in a jealous rage, but he would never hurt my sister!"

She looked over at Brian and watched the relief fill his eyes. She knew instantly that he was not relieved at the effect it might have on the judge or jury but relieved that she believed it to be true.

He hadn't lost Brenda entirely. Brenda was fighting for him. He had been forgiven.

Brenda looked back at Brian as he stood defeated and disgraced. His misery on display for the entertainment and pleasure of those he used to call his friends.

His eyes met hers and she wished with every morsel of her existence that she had never lit the touchpaper to this heinous shitshow.

Brian lifted his eyes to meet hers and her heart fell further into the abyss.

There was no hatred. No anger. No bitterness.

She too, had been forgiven.

Franks parents, having travelled from Australia back to the place they had once fled in a hurricane of fear, had sat through the whole trial without once showing any emotion. They sat numbly in their seats. Listening to the unfolding story of how their son met his untimely death.

Brian watched them constantly. His remorse and regret spilling from his face as they continued to avert their eyes from the man who had stolen their one remaining child. Their brave son who had taken this boy under his wing in school, who'd had the courage to return to the girl he loved and paid the ultimate price for it. Not at the hands of those they expected but at the hands of his schoolfriend! Up until a few months ago they had believed Frank to have fallen victim to another vicious attack from his own grandfather and that had somehow seemed easier to bear. A consequence of their lives of crime but this? This seemed so incredibly pointless.

Brian was imagining their pain. After losing one child, the lengths they had gone to in order to protect Frank had been remarkable. They had left everything at a moment's notice to start a new life at the other side of the world and their son, in pursuit of his teenage sweetheart, had fallen foul, not to the gang members they feared, but to this unassuming, mild-mannered man who used to be his friend.

The jury returned their guilty verdict on both counts. A double murder and as the courtroom cleared, Frank's mother gave Brenda a cordial nod. It wasn't a nod of approval but the acknowledgment that she was also an innocent victim of the whole tragic debacle. They returned home to Australia without waiting for the sentencing as nothing here felt relevant to them now. Both Brian and Brenda independently acknowledged the heart-breaking irony of it. Franks parents were leaving behind their one remaining offspring. The granddaughter they never knew they had.

Two weeks later at the sentencing the judge handed down a sentence of sixteen years. It was light for the crimes, but Brenda felt no relief in it.

"You did everything you could for him. It's down to you that he got off so lightly." Sheila whispered as the courtroom started to clear.

Brenda listened but she wasn't buying it. The lack of a second body had played a huge part in the sentence and the fact that he'd been provoked into a frenzy of jealousy had also contributed to the judge realising that Brian was no danger to the public. She was convinced of that.

The only thing that was down to her, was the fact that he would be out of their lives for sixteen long years. The loving father who helped Frankie with her maths and chemistry, the funny, sweet man who filled the other half of her empty bed.

She took Sheila's arm and left that building with the stark realisation that, when it came to stabbing oneself in the foot, she had driven the spade right through it. Chopping off her ability to move forward in any direction. She was bleeding out.

"Will you take Frankie to visit him?"

"Do you think she'd want to go?" Brenda replied. "Her father has just been locked away for the murder of her mother!"

Sheila patted the hand that was looped through her arm.

"Frankie isn't that stupid. She might still have strong memories of Amelia, but she totally knows Brian. She won't believe it for a minute."

And Sheila was right. As always.

Frankie was desperate for contact with her dad, but Brenda was reluctant to start up regular visits to Strangeways with a ten-year-old girl.

"It's no place for a child. Maybe when you're a bit older, Frankie."

"He'll forget who I am by then. He won't know anything about me. I want to see him now. Right now!"

Brenda knew she had a point and that her own reluctance to face Brian again was playing a heavy role in her decision. She was also desperate to relieve her own guilt in denying Frankie contact with the father who would still be with her every day, had it not been from that moment of madness when she strutted to the police station without thinking it through.

Then, as Brenda tried to find a compromise between Frankie's need to visit and her own need to stay away, the answer came in the form of Charlie and Jean Gilbert. Brian's parents turned up on the doorstep asking if they could take Frankie to see their son.

Brenda invited them in and both parties felt instantly relieved at the lack of animosity.

"Our son did wrong and it's right that he should pay for it." Brian's father said firmly.

"But that doesn't mean Frankie should suffer too." His mother added.

Brenda couldn't have agreed more and immediately called Frankie down to give her the news.

Frankie beamed and hugged her and then she hugged Jean who promised to get a visiting order as soon as possible and the order arrived for a Saturday a few weeks later.

Frankie was excited on the morning of the visit and asked Brenda to braid her hair into a French plait. She picked out a dress which Brenda replaced with a shell suit, and she picked out a pair of sparkly sandals which Brenda replaced with trainers.

After she'd been collected, Sheila and Brenda went into town to try to take their minds of it. Frankie had run to the car with her newly braided hair trailing to her waist and a huge smile on her face but Brenda felt nervous about the whole thing as she stood at the market stall unable to concentrate on what to have for dinner at all.

"It's going to be a huge shock for her to see him in a prison uniform." she sighed as she handed over the money for the potatoes she'd absent-mindedly put in her bag.

"Frankie is a strong girl. She'll be so happy to see Brian again, she won't even notice!" Sheila assured.

But Sheila's words fell far short of assurance. The only words that registered was the happiness of the reunion of father and daughter and for that, she felt the guilt all over again.

In one fell swoop, she'd removed Brian from their lives without considering that she could never fill his huge shoes. He'd been much more than a father. He was her homework buddy, her partner in many cheeky crimes, her port in a storm and her best friend.

"Stop blaming yourself!" Sheila scolded.

"I wasn't!"

"Yes you were." Sheila argued. "The man is a murderer!"

"But is he though?" Brenda asked, "didn't he just have a simple moment of tragic desperation?"

Sheila simply patted her hand without responding and steered her back towards the carpark.

Back at home the kettle had only just boiled when Charlie Gilbert's car drew up.

The couple walked her to the door and waited until it opened before returning to their car.

Frankie was beaming from ear to ear.

"Dad has made lots of new friends and he's enrolled on a cookery course! He says he's going to learn to cook dinner parties for when he gets out."

Sheila raised her eyebrows and smiled.

"I take it you'll be going to see him again then?"

"Yes, and next time I'm taking my maths book so he can see where I am and get the same book out of his library. We can work together, and he says I'll definitely get into the top class when I move up to secondary school!"

Brenda felt a little of her guilt start to lift. Not all had been lost.

She watched Frankie's excited eyes as the stories of prison gushed from her lips and the promises Brian had made danced behind them.

She knew Brian would keep every promise he'd made because that's who he was and that's why she still loved him.

She hugged Frankie close and kissed the top of her black braids as she considered that, at last, a small glimmer of silver lining had appeared around the biggest black cloud of their lives.

Chapter 9

The positive impact of Frankie's visits to see Brian had such a huge impact on alleviating Brenda's guilt that she welcomed every opportunity.

She listened intently to the snippets of Brian's life and tried to imagine his funny expressions as he told their little girl about his antics.

Things almost started to feel normal again. So normal that she started to consider visiting him herself if only to hear him speak again. The truth of the matter was that she missed him terribly and hearing of him second-hand no longer felt enough.

Then Frankie got the news that she had got into the top class at school, and it seemed like the perfect time to touch base with Brian and to thank him for his efforts.

She called Jean to let her know that she was going to apply for a visiting order and tag along on the next visit since 3 adults were allowed with a child.

"Oh. We were thinking of missing the next one to be honest. Maybe you would like to take Frankie on your own?"

Brenda felt a little taken aback. It seemed like Jean was trying to give them some space together.

"Yes, of course. Thank you."

She put the receiver down and went over the conversation again. Jean seemed to have been caught off guard but maybe she was just surprised and made up an excuse to allow her son to re-connect with her.

She applied for the visiting order and the following Saturday two letters dropped on the mat.

The first was from the prison and the second bore the stamp of a solicitor.

She opened the prison visiting order which had been approved and then turned her attention to the second letter.

She opened it up chewing a mouthful of toast until she managed to absorb the content. She stopped chewing and held it before her eyes as she walked to Sheila's door and entered without knocking.

Sheila was sitting up in bed with a book in her hand when she looked up to find Brenda motionless at the foot of her bed, still holding the letter in front of her eyes.

"What is it, Brenda? What's happened?"

Brenda looked up from the paper and frowned before looking back at it as though checking she'd read it correctly.

"Its Jean and Charlie. They've applied for full custody of Frankie!"

"What! Why would they do that?"

"I have no idea, but they are petitioning on the grounds that Amelia is presumed dead, and Frankie's father incarcerated so, as grandparents they believe they can provide a more stable environment than an aunt and an elderly woman with less claim over the child.!"

"They won't win, Brenda."

"Damn right they won't!"

She stormed out of the room and within seconds Sheila could hear her screaming down the phone, presumably to Jean.

"You scheming bitch! After I allowed you to take her to see Brian! I thought we were trying to build her life back up, not tear it apart! Well, you can forget ever picking her up again. In fact, you can just fuck off!"

She slammed down the receiver and returned to Sheila.

"Well, that was diplomatic!" Sheila grinned. "Classy!"

Brenda burst out laughing.

"Tea and toast?"

"Yes please."

Sheila got out of bed and got herself dressed before heading for the kitchen but before she'd managed to take a sip of the tea there was a hammering at the door.

"I'll get it!" Brenda snapped, already anticipating the scene that was about to unfold.

She opened the door and Jean barged in without waiting to be invited. Her wiry greying hair standing out from her head as though it hadn't seen a comb this morning.

"Oh, do come in." Brenda said sarcastically.

Charlie walked obediently but uncomfortably behind with his hair carefully combed over to cover his bald patch.

"I don't know who you think you are, young lady but I'm not easily threatened! Our solicitor says we have an excellent chance of getting Frankie, so you better watch your step if you want any access to her at all!"

"Is that right?" Brenda smiled.

"Yes, it is!" She hissed directly into Brenda's face. Her bulbous eyes, only inches away, with her thin lined lips tense to the point of almost disappearing entirely.

Brenda then sat down and took a sip from her cup. She'd been waiting for this acrimonious invasion since the moment she'd replaced the receiver and she was determined to savour every moment of it.

Jean pulled up a chair and sat opposite as Brenda took a bite of her toast and washed it down with another sip of tea.

"We are Frankie's grandparents and we have rights!

"Are you sure about that?"

"Of course we are sure! Our solicitor told us about grandparents rights!"

"Not that bit. The other bit." Brenda said calmly, smugly.

"What!"

"The grandparents bit. Are you sure about that?"

"Of course we are sure. What are you saying!"

"I'm saying that perhaps you should have spoken to your son before you set these particular hares racing."

"What makes you think we haven't?"

"Oh! I know you haven't because Brian would have told you to back off!"

"Why would he?"

Suddenly, Sheila's face changed. Her eyes widened as though warning Brenda not to cross that line but Brenda was in full swing and no-one was going to prevent her from delivering the punch line.

"Because," Brenda said calmly

Sheila was frantically shaking her head.

"Because Brian is not Frankie's father, and any blood test will prove that!"

The scuttling from behind, prevented anyone from responding.

Brenda spun around to catch a glimpse of Frankie hurtling out of the door and onto the street.

"I tried to warn you!" Sheila screamed. "Get after her!"

Brenda was out of the front door and in pursuit within a few seconds while Sheila simply folded her arms and huffed.

"I suggest you leave now. Go and speak to your son and then decide what you want to do. This was not a good move on your part. Not good at all."

Jean's anger and frustration was causing her to tremble as she pushed back the chair and marched to the door but Charlie was neither of those things. Sheila could see from his demeanour that he was neither suspicious about the claim nor angry about the years of deceit. He was simply devastated and saddened that he had just lost a much-loved granddaughter.

Sheila also felt the pain of it as she closed the door on the couple who were about to abandon Frankie completely.

Out on the street, Brenda was no match for Frankie as she tripped along in fluffy mule slippers but she wasn't worried. She knew exactly where Frankie would be heading. She would catch up with her at that sacred clearing in the woods. The place where her mother would find solace. The place she had often lain with her niece and told her every story of Amelia that she could remember.

As she entered the clearing and the light shone down through the trees like a huge spotlight on some grand stage, her heart sank with dread at the nature of the play that was about to be performed.

Today, Frankie was not lying on her back staring at the clouds but sobbing into the ground.

Brenda padded over on blooded bare feet with her slippers in her hand and sank down beside her.

"I'm so sorry you heard that, Frankie."

Frankie continued to sob without acknowledging.

Brenda reached out her hands and collected the splayed black hair that had fallen either side of her waist. Once captured, she stroked it affectionately through her closed fists, allowing it to fall from one hand to the other.

Eventually the sobbing ebbed away and Frankie spoke without moving from her position.

"Is it true?"

Brenda sighed.

She didn't need to answer because Frankie knew that sigh well.

She sat up and thrust herself into Brenda's arms.

"I'm so sorry." Brenda repeated. "I wish I could fix this but I can't."

She felt Frankie nod against her chest.

They remained in the embrace for several seconds before Frankie eventually pulled away and levelled her puffy reddened eyes with those of her surrogate mother. The only parent she had left.

"Who is my real father then?"

She heard that sigh again and her heart skipped a beat.

Brenda knew she couldn't prolong this agony for the little girl she loved more than life itself.

"Your biological father was a boy your mum met in school."

"What happened to him? Did they break up?"

This time Brenda denied the sigh that was aching to be released.

"His parents took him away suddenly for his own safety. He didn't know your mum was pregnant with you."

Brenda watched the frown on Frankie's face as her mind started to build the picture of a story she'd heard before. The story that her friends had repeated from the newspapers.

"Was my father Frank? Frank Palmer?" She asked suddenly.

Brenda pulled her close again and nodded against the top of her head.

She felt Frankie sobbing again and held her tightly until there were no tears left.

"Come on. Let's get you home. Sheila will be worried."

The words home and Sheila had been a deliberate attempt to offer comfort and it seemed to work.

Frankie pulled herself up and snaked her arm around Brenda's waist to start the walk back home.

"Your feet are bleeding." She said as she sniffed back the tears.

"Well, you did tell me I ought to have bought the full slippers with the rabbit ears!" Brenda smiled.

They walked along the path in silence for a while and then Frankie suddenly seemed to regain her composure and spoke clearly and calmly.

"Daddy killed my real father."

"Yes, he did."

"He did it because he thought we were going to leave him."

"Yes, he did. Does this mean you don't want to visit him in prison anymore."

"I don't know."

She went silent for a while.

" My real father came back for mummy and then found out about me then?"

"Yes."

"And daddy killed him? Before he even saw me?"

"Yes he did ....but he was only trying to..."

"To keep us apart. Yes, I know and now I will never meet my real father!"

Chapter 10

The following week Brenda travelled alone on the train to visit Brian.

She entered the table-ridden hall and scanned around the sea of faces all dressed in identical blue shirts until her eyes fell on the thin pock-marked face of the man she'd betrayed.

Brian rose to his feet slightly as she approached and greeted her with a melancholy smile. Suddenly, she was overwhelmed by his unfaltering good manners.

She returned his smile, before pulling out the chair opposite and lowering herself into it.

The tone had been set.

This was not going to be a confrontation but a reunion of two people who had more feelings for one another than she ever imagined.

She studied his weathered face. This was the first time she'd been alone with him since the morning she'd kissed him goodbye and then calmly sealed his fate with the delivery of that case.

"I'm an idiot." Was her opening line.

Brian grinned.

"No. I'm the idiot."

"You don't deserve to be here, Brian."

"We both know that's not true."

He reached for her hand and she allowed him to take it. A guard frowned but didn't intervene as their hands remained cradled.

"You are the one who made me realise that I was never in love with your sister. With Amelia." He said softly.

"But I thought… I thought she was everything to you!"

Brian shook his head.

"I thought so too. I thought my world was about to end if she left with Frank, but I was wrong."

"But you killed Frank!"

"I know. It was the biggest mistake anyone could have made. I panicked. I couldn't bear to watch my family walk away but all of that changed the moment I saw you dragging your worldly possessions over that carpark in London. Cursing and swearing after finding that Lawrence bloke in bed with a young girl."

"I remember it well." Brenda sighed.

"I remember it well too. It was the moment my heart melted. It was so comical and yet so tragic. I just wanted to scoop you up and take care of you forever. I fell in love with you in the time it took for you to drag those damn cases to my car."

Brenda shook her head in dismay.

"You probably won't believe this, but it was on that journey home that I began to realise what a wonderful man my sister had married. You had come to my rescue and somehow I was already envying Amelia for having you by her side."

He squeezed her hand across the table.

"It seems like we both fell in love at the same time."

They both allowed the suggestion to marinate for a second. To resonate and be considered before it settled in it's rightful place of their history.

Without doubt, they had fallen in love that day.

"Don't get me wrong," Brian added, "I did care deeply for Amelia and I had always felt so damn lucky that fate had delivered a girl into my arms. Any girl, because I never expected to get one but what I had with Amelia was bordering on fantasy. We were living our lives with the painted smiles of actors. I can see that now. We were living under the threatening cloud of another stroke of fate. The potential return of Frank. Amelia's real love. Frankie's real father."

Everything Brian was saying was true, but Brenda had never seen it that way before.

She reciprocated the hand squeeze and Brian closed his fingers more tightly around that soft hand he'd held in bed a thousand times.

"Frank had been my friend." He said softly. "He'd included me in a way no-one else in that school ever had and look what I did to him! I should have let him go. Taken his family and made a new life for them all. I'd never really had Amelia, after all. I'd just been taking care of her and Frankie for him. Everything could have been so different. We could have stayed in touch, and I could have had holidays in Oz, couldn't I? Been the uncle who visited. The hero who'd stepped up and done what was right by his best friend. It all seems so clear sitting in that cell for hours on end. I can see why incarceration works. It forces you to go over things again and again until you finally get it!"

"But at the time all you could see was that you were about to lose your wife and child."

Brian gave a little false laugh.

"No. Frank's wife and child. I knew things weren't right between us. I knew her heart was always floating out there somewhere, searching for her real husband and I don't blame her. Frank was a wonderful guy. Smart, stunning and hilariously funny. I could have married him myself."

"Fate has been so unkind to you." She soothed.

"Unkind! Unkind?" His eyes widened. "I hit my best mate on the head that morning for the sake of a woman and then fell in love with another woman that very night! Unkind is a bit of an under-statement don't you think?"

His synopsis caused her to stifle a chuckle. Her attempt to contain it caused him to chuckle and within a second they both gave way to spontaneous laughter.

It reminded her of the laughter at his wedding to Amelia. The release of so many pent-up emotions that had suddenly found a fissure through which to escape.

The unbelievable irony of it. The heart-wrenching tragedy of it and the total pointlessness of it all.

Tears of laughter merged with tears of despair as they turned every head in that room.

Then their laughter faded away as their hands remained joined and Brenda reached over to wipe away his tears.

"I love you, Brian Gilbert. I'm going to do everything I can to fix this."

"Well, its not like I'm going anywhere." He smiled.

"It doesn't matter. I'll wait for you."

Brian shook his head.

"Look at you!" He stroked her blonde waves back over her shoulder. "You're stunning. Any man would be lucky to have you and you have your entire life still ahead of you."

She stroked his face again and stood up to leave.

"I don't need just any man. I need you."

Brian smiled at the naivety of her parting statement as she rose from her seat to leave. He knew that her feelings were genuine, but he also knew that many men would come into her life in the years to come. Men stricken by her beauty, captivated by her warm heart and compelled, just as he had been, to protect her.

As she trailed her hand in his until their fingers fell apart, he could feel her commitment and determination to stand by him but soon that promise would be broken as inevitably as the touch of those fingers.

Brenda's heart was breaking as she joined the bunch of bodies waiting to exit the visiting room. She wished they would hurry up and get the hell out of that door so that she didn't have to keep that smile frozen on her face.

As soon as she was out of sight, the tears came.

She walked to the carpark around the corner and sat behind the wheel without starting the engine.

She had to do whatever she could to alleviate the suffering she'd caused. To Brian, to Frankie, to Barry and to Sheila. Each of them had lost the love of a person who'd brought them such joy until she stole it away with her stupidity. No good had come of Brian's conviction. Not for anyone and certainly not for Frank or Amelia, wherever she was.

As she drove back along the M62 she was mapping out her plan of atonement.

She would speak to Frankie and somehow persuade her that Brian was still the loving father she's always believed him to be. The dad who used to sleep beside her in that single bed when she had the flu. The dad who was never too busy to play chess with her or teach her how to change spark plugs. The one who always showed up at school plays and open days even when Amelia didn't make it. Even when Brenda didn't make it.

She sighed and moved into the slow lane to recover from the reality that Brian had been a better parent than either Amelia or herself.

She turned her attention to fixing the relationship between Barry and Sheila. By Christmas, they would both be back at the family table, bickering and laughing together. She was aware that Sheila's heart had always been waiting for her father to fill it, but she also knew that Barry had done a pretty good job of occupying it with his own brand of love. An occupancy that had, without doubt, satiated the emptiness and filled it with affection and joy.

She tried to visualise how she wanted things to be.

Weekly visits to the prison with Frankie who would gush her news to Brian who would regain his position as her father. He would co-parent with letters and phone calls whenever he could, and they would soon start to look forward to the day when he would return to the family home. She tried to see it. To visualise her goal just as Amelia used to tell her to.

"See it in your mind's eye and it will happen." Her sister used to say whenever she lost confidence in herself but today, Amelia was not there to guide her.

Amelia would know what to do. Amelia would fix whatever could be fixed.

As she loitered in the slow lane, she had never felt less capable of anything. Suddenly, she felt more like a child than an adult. A child who needed Sheila's arms around her as desperately as she needed that reassuring smile from her big sister.

She banged her fist on the steering wheel in rage and turned her head to the sky above.

"Where are you Mealy! Where the fuck are you!"

Cars started to honk around her as she drifted from one lane to another with her eyes fixed on the empty sky until she moved out into the fast lane and slammed her foot to the floor.

She had to get home and rid herself of this guilt and the only way to do that was to repair as much of the damage as she could.

That's what Mealy would do.

Chapter 11

"But he killed my father, didn't he? My real dad?" Frankie protested when Brenda arrived home and opened up the conversation.

"Yes, he did and that was a bad thing. But sometimes people do bad things because they are just so frightened." Brenda replied.

The conversation with Frankie was not going well.

"Frightened of what?"

"Of losing you, of course. Frank Palmer had come here for one reason and that was to take you and your mummy away from him."

She'd purposely used Frank's real name to alienate him from his parental status.

"But the paper's all said that he was mummy's boyfriend, and she was going to run off and take me away from my dad but that wasn't true, was it? He wasn't just her old boyfriend; he was my dad. Nobody said that!"

Brenda listened and marvelled at several elements of her niece's response. Firstly, she noticed how she referred to Frank as her dad the way most ten-year-olds would, but when she spoke of Amelia, she used the word an infant would use. Amelia was always referred to as 'mummy' because she'd disappeared without ever being progressed to 'mum.' She also marvelled at Frankie's grasp on the secret that had been withheld from the courts.

"You're right." Brenda sighed. "Nobody knows that but Frank hadn't been seen for so many years and your dad took you both on. He married your mum and loved you more than most dad's ever love their children. He just loved you so much and couldn't bear to lose you."

She could see Frankie's eyes starting to fill up. Frankie hated to argue with Brenda, but she was feeling frustrated and confused. She started raking her fingers through her long black hair and Brenda could see the loose hairs that were starting to accumulate in her fist. This was Frankie's way of dealing with anxiety.

Brenda instantly pulled her close and placed her hand over the hand that was trying to drag out her beautiful hair.

"Don't worry about it, love." She soothed. "You don't have to visit the prison if you don't want to. Everything is going to be alright."

"I think," she said, as she tried to stifle a sob. "that my real dad came back for us as soon as he could. To take us away to a beautiful place with a big garden."

Brenda couldn't argue with that.

It was exactly what had happened, and Frank Palmer had done nothing wrong. He'd returned for Amelia without ever knowing that he also had a daughter waiting for him or that his best friend had married the mother of his child. Frank was not to blame here. Frank didn't deserve to die.

Frankie continued to rake at her hair until Brenda gently placed her hand over the offending fist.

"Mummy didn't go without me, did she?"

"No, love. She would never do that."

"Where is she then?"

Brenda couldn't inflict Amelia's fanciful account of her missing year in some half-way house between this life and the next on a ten-year-old so she simply shrugged.

"I don't know love. I really don't"

"I think she didn't come back because she's dead." Frankie said firmly.

"I think my dad killed her too."

Brenda pulled her close.

"Isn't that what you think auntie Bren?"

Brenda allowed the question to go unanswered for a while. Something she had never done before even though she'd heard the accusation a hundred times. Rejected it a hundred times. Denied that Brian was capable of ever hurting her sister.

The silence began to speak for itself.

Her tightened grip on her niece was transmitting an unprecedented whisper of doubt and with that doubt grew the devastating possibility that she might have been blinded by her love for Brian.

That the body of her sister was lying undiscovered in a shallow grave somewhere.

The shudder surged through both of them, causing Brenda to break the bodily contact.

"I don't know what to think darling but I just don't believe that your dad would do that."

"But you don't know for sure?"

"No, I don't." Brenda sighed.

That night, after Frankie went to bed she sat down to write the letter that would extinguish all hope of ever reuniting her family.

After sealing it and addressing it to the prison, she put it on the mantle and stared at it for hours.

Inside that small innocent looking envelope lay the words that would tear Brian's heart into a thousand pieces. The news that his little girl doubted his innocence. That Brenda was trying desperately not to share those doubts.

That she needed to put her own feelings for him aside and protect their little girl.

She would not be visiting again.

She allowed that envelope to taunt her from that mantle for many hours. Watching it as though it was about to pounce. Wondering if it would soon make its way to the post-box or be ripped into a hundred pieces and slammed into the bin.

Moments of torturous indecision were not alien to her and she knew that eventually something deep inside her would intervene. Some parental voice that would put an end to the squabbling and make the decision swiftly, with its no-nonsense finality.

Just after midnight, she was sure that she felt her heart take its' last breath as she allowed that letter to fall from her fingers into the post-box at the end of the street.

She walked numbly home, crawled into bed, pulled the covers over her head and sobbed.

A few days later she was sitting with Sheila when another letter fell onto the mat.

A letter that said so little that it said everything.

'My darling. I totally understand. Frankie is more important than either of us. Look after our little girl. My only hope is that one day Amelia will come home. All my love, forever. Brian.'

She read it and then passed it to Sheila who wiped away a tear and then pulled herself up to full sitting height by hoisting up her breasts with folded arms and blowing the air from her lungs.

"That's that then." She said heartily. "Time for a change I think. I'll put my cottage on the market, you can do the same with this place and we'll make an offer on that big house you've always been obsessed with."

"What big house?"

"I saw the estates agent's sign last week. That bloody house I always had to fetch you and Amelia back from when you were either sitting outside of it or circling the drive on your scruffy bikes!"

"It's up for sale?"

"Yep and if we both put our houses on the market at a bargain price we could sell quickly and still afford it."

"Have you been planning this?"

"I might have." Sheila laughed. "Here's the brochure. I think we all need a new start, don't you?"

Brenda felt her heart begin to stir. It wasn't jumping for joy or filling back up with hope but it was a start. She could feel the beginning of some sort of recovery starting to creep into her soul.

A life with Sheila and Frankie in that house was giving her a strange feeling of contentment.

At the time she believed it was nothing other than the peace of mind that comes with making a decision and of realising that there are worse things than to make a life with two people you love.

It was only after moving into that house that she realised her glimmer of joy and hope were coming from somewhere else entirely.

Only after the removal men had left and she took the time to sit at her new bedroom window with a large glass of housewarming wine did she realise where that glimmer was peeping from.

She smiled at the large tree in the centre of the drive and then allowed her eyes to follow the tarmac back to the huge gates onto the lane.

Her eyes remained fixed on those gates as they would for many years to come.

She took a sip of the cold wine, and an involuntary whisper came from her lips.

"Come on Mealy, I'm waiting, where are you?"

Chapter 12

Brenda's hope served them well.

As they settled into that new house it was with a hint of optimism that someday everything would be alright again.

It was the year in which they would re-align their positions in this new family, quietly re-establish their routines and gently accept each other's private heartache.

It was a time of mutual support but also a time of private reflection and Sheila seemed to be the only one to feel concerned by the new dynamic.

It wasn't until Frankie left junior school in the summer of 1987 that she decided to speak out.

"I think we need to speak to Frankie, Bren."

Brenda was arranging a freshly cut pile of roses into a vase.

"I can't believe the size of these roses." Brenda exclaimed without acknowledging Sheila's blemish on her good mood. "This garden is perfect for roses." She continued as she shook another free from the pile on the worktop.

"Did you hear what I said?"

"Yes, I heard you, but I don't know why you're trying to spoil my morning. Frankie is fine."

"You know that's not true. She didn't do very well in her exams and when she starts her new school in September she needs to concentrate. She's a bright girl. She used to be top of the class when…."

"When Brian was here?" Brenda snapped.

"Yes," Sheila sighed, "when Brian was here."

"He used to coach her, that's why. Perhaps she'd benefit from a few private maths lessons or something."

"You know it's more than that, Bren."

Brenda sighed.

"What do you want me to do? Drag her to the prison against her will for tutoring?"

"Of course not. I just think it's time we spoke to her about her mother. About Amelia."

"Don't you think she's already had enough to deal with?"

"Yes, I do but I also think that she isn't really dealing with it at all. She's full of questions without answers."

"You think that hearing about Amelia's ridiculous stories would actually be a comfort, do you!"

"I've seen you sitting in your window staring at that gate, Bren. You don't believe for a minute that Amelia is dead. You don't believe that Brian could ever hurt her and Amelia's account of what happened might seem insane but it's what she believed. Frankie deserves to know the truth because the truth is better than the horrors she's imagining."

Brenda snipped a rose far too short and threw it into the sink.

"I thought we were doing alright." She said more softly.

"I know." Sheila walked over and placed a hand on her shoulder. "But we aren't. Not really. Frankie has a missing mother and an incarcerated dad. You are spending every minute of every day waiting for Amelia to walk back into our lives and complete this family again and I, well I am just walking on eggshells, watching my girls going through the motions of life without feeling it."

"You think we should tell her about the day Amelia returned with the milk? About her story of being gone for just a few minutes? Don't you think that will push her over the edge?"

"No, I think it might pull her back from it."

Brenda hadn't felt the thorn pierce her finger until Sheila's hand thrust it under the tap.

"Alright. Let's talk to her when she gets back from dance class."

Sheila smiled and started to clip the rest of the stalks.

Later that evening it was Brenda who started the conversation about Amelia's strange re-appearance.

"Do you remember anything about it?" She asked as Frankie finished off her pudding.

"I don't know. I remember coming home in the car after a sleepover and being so excited that mummy was home and then being told that she wasn't."

"Yes." Brenda soothed. "That was awful for you. You were far too young to understand what really happened and even now… well, we don't understand it either!"

Frankie frowned as Brenda started to recount the events of that notorious day.

Sheila kept her arm around Frankie's shoulders as though trying to support her as the story unfolded.

Frankie's eyes remained firmly on Brenda's as though she was checking for some indication that this was a joke, but her expression remained fixed and devoid of emotion right until Brenda heaved a sigh and stopped talking.

"Are you alright, love?" Sheila squeezed her shoulders.

Frankie simply nodded and remained silent as the two women watched her intently.

Her eyes shifted back and forth as she processed the information and then she finally spoke.

"Do you think it's possible?" She asked. "Do you think she was telling the truth?"

"I believe that she believed it." Brenda replied.

"But do you think it's possible?"

"I really don't know love."

She then turned to Sheila.

"Do you think it is?"

Sheila smiled.

"I think there are many things in this world, and probably in the next, of which we all know very little."

"So, you think it might be true."

"I think it's possible."

"You think my mummy just walked into my father's world that was some place between the living and the dead and that she came back and a whole year had gone?"

Sheila shrugged.

Brenda sat down at the other side of Frankie and rested her head on top of the shiny black, poker-straight curtain of hair. Sheila watched Brenda's pearly white waves cascade like the icing on a Christmas cake and marvelled, as she had many times, at the bond between this mother and daughter that biology had played no part in.

"What are you thinking?" Brenda whispered.

Frankie stiffened.

"I'm thinking that everyone had gone fucking mad!" She exclaimed comically.

"Frankie Gilbert!" Sheila bellowed. "Language!"

Suddenly, everyone laughed.

The ice that had thickened over several years had finally been broken.

It no longer mattered who was right or wrong or if Amelia had been deluded and lost or confused and absconded.

What mattered was that there were no secrets in this family anymore. They all shared the same information now and it was up to each of them to consider it, discuss it and deal with it as a family.

Finally, they were all on the same side.

In September of 1987 Frankie started her new school and immediately seemed to be doing better.

Sometimes they spoke of the mystery of Amelia's disappearance and always they concluded that the house contained three open minds.

"Do you even remember your mummy?" Brenda asked during one such debate.

"Sometimes I think I do but then I wonder if it's just that I've seen the photos of us together and matched them to the stories."

"But you remember coming home that morning excited to see her again?"

"Yes! Yes I still remember that and I also think I remember her smelly wet coat."

Sheila laughed. "She never left it out to dry. She always put it right back on the hook. I was always telling her!"

"I do remember something else though. Well, I think I do."

"What?" Sheila asked.

"I think that we used to hold hands… like this." She threaded her fingers through Sheila's and immediately Brenda reacted.

"You did! You did that a lot with her."

Frankie tapped Sheila's fingers one by one as she sang..

"My black cat can play the piano, my black cat can play the piano."

Brenda could barely see for the tears. She'd totally forgotten how Amelia and Frankie used to sit singing that song as they tapped each finger in turn when Frankie couldn't sleep.

"You remember her, Frankie! You remember her."

Frankie smiled.

"She used to make those hand shadows on the wall after our story. Rabbits, owls and spiders and sometimes we used to sing that song about holding hands with a power so divine, even though I didn't know what divine meant."

"You are my world by Cilla Black!" Brenda muttered quietly.

"Then we used to play 'what time is it Mr Wolf' when we waited for dad to come home and in the summer, she let me paint the path with a paint brush and water."

Brenda hadn't witnessed any of that, but she recognised it. They were the things their own mother had done with them. The legacy of Celia Simpson.

Brenda pushed Frankie back to arm's length and smiled.

"That sounds exactly like your mum. Of course, you remember her."

"I think we need to find her." Frankie announced as though it was a case of taking a look around the block.

"You think we haven't tried?" Sheila laughed.

"I don't know. Have you?"

"Of course, we have." Brenda assured. "I think it's up to her to find her way home now."

Frankie shrugged her disagreement and turned on the tv.

As Sheila and Brenda washed the dishes, Frankie's words hung heavily in the air.

"Have we, Sheila? Have we really tried to find her?"

"You mean have we looked in places the eye can't see?"

"Yep."

Sheila sighed.

"It's a dangerous game."

"Yes. Probably better left alone."

They washed and dried the pots in silence before returning to the living room where Frankie was engrossed in an episode of the Gladiators.

"I like Wolf the best." She announced as the wild-haired Gladiator growled at the camera. "He's determined and fearless."

Sheila and Brenda exchanged a glance. The intimation had not been lost on them. Frankie was accusing them of being to cowardly to find her mummy and urging them to make a start.

After Frankie went to bed, Brenda opened the conversation.

"You know what Frankie meant?"

"I do."

"Do you think she's right?"

"That we should go poking around in the unknown?"

"Yes, that?"

Sheila took on an air of sudden authority.

"Until this happened to Amelia, I had no idea of how many people go missing in this world without ever coming home and I'm pretty sure they're not all buried in ditches. Amelia is a strong, determined mother. If there was a way, she would find it. Frankie doesn't need us two disappearing down the rabbit hole as well!"

Brenda felt the relief of Sheila's words.

"We stay put and wait?"
"We stay put and wait." Sheila repeated. "And pray."

Chapter 13

In the autumn Frankie started her new school and a different world opened to her.

Suddenly she was getting attention from boys in the years above her. Boys who were bursting with ego, and high on the newly surging testosterone they found difficult to contain. Frankie was painfully aware that her striking good looks usually attracted attention, but she was not prepared for the juvenile, disrespectful and vulgar way in which these boys tended to make their point.

Mostly she tried to ignore it. Sometimes she would retaliate with a smart remark and on more than one occasion, she delivered a well-earned slap in the face, but her reactions served only to stoke the flames. She became known as the bitch, the dragon, or the frigid lesbian, causing some girls to alienate her but a few others to stand by her in rigid solidarity.

Something was happening inside that neither she, nor Brenda or Sheila were aware of.

Deep in her psyche, she was forming an opinion of the male gender based on her entire experience of every male she had ever known.

Of the dad she had trusted so completely who had been revealed as a murderer. The man who had probably killed her own mother! Of Barry who she knew little about other than the fact that he had betrayed Sheila to the extent that she no longer had anything to do with him. Of her grandad who had broken Sheila's heart and of whom she still spoke regularly. Of the herd of boys who taunted her with their disgusting innuendos.

Frankie was very quickly gravitating towards her female teachers. Biology, Religion and Social studies became her favourite lessons.

Frankie was becoming a man-hater.

But her gravitation was opening up yet another, more positive world which allowed her to study the function of the brain, the behaviour of the mind and the crucial question as to whether a life beyond this one actually existed.

Frankie's hunger for knowledge wasn't driven by the desire for top marks but the desire to solve the mystery of her missing mother.

She frequented the school library, asking for books on every element of the brain, the mind and the afterlife but she was careful never to reveal her intentions. She knew better than to add insanity to the arsenal of her tormentors.

Sometimes a group of them would press their faces to the library window and gesture to her but she'd learned to ignore them. She would sit on her chair with her legs loosely crossed, her top button slightly open and her silky black hair draped over one shoulder and disguise a smile. She recognised their bitterness for exactly what it was. Sheer frustration. Like infants, they craved attention. Good or bad. They just wanted a reaction because the crux of the matter was that they longed to possess her.

She turned a page and recrossed her long legs.

She was the one with the power here!

At home, she would interrogate Brenda and Sheila often. Asking for details of her mother. Dates, times, places and her demeanour. About her relationship with Frank Palmer and how Brian came onto the scene.

The two women tried to appease her by trying to recall facts that they had barely committed to memory. Facts that they now think they should have paid more attention to.

Then, during one such grilling, when Brenda was barely concentrating on her answers, a sentence popped out of her mouth that flipped open the lid on the can of worms they'd pledged never to open.

"Brian was fascinated by the mind-reading I believe."

"What mind-reading!"

Brenda stared at the face that was already staring back at her.

"What mind-reading!"

Brenda felt her face burning as the blood rushed to colour it red. She needed to play it down, and quickly.

"Oh, your mum and Frank used to pretend to read each other's minds. It was a prank that's all."

"Why would my dad be fascinated by a prank? I don't believe you!"

Frankie ran up to her room.

Brenda took a deep breath and then followed.

"I'm sorry Frankie. You're right. They used to try to guess what each other was thinking and sometimes they said they'd got it right."

"Tell her the truth." Sheila's voice came from the doorway.

"Just tell her the truth. She's not a baby anymore."

Sheila entered the room and plonked herself on the bed beside Frankie.

"It started with your mummy and auntie Brenda actually."

Sheila hardly ever referred to Brenda as anything other than mum and it felt suddenly cold to Frankie. A stark reminder that her real mummy had just demoted her stand-in.

"You did it too?"

"Only for a little while. We used to do it just before we went to sleep. It was like a game." Brenda admitted.

"Did it work?"

"Sometimes I think it did but then Frank came along, and he was much better at it than me, apparently."

Frankie's desolation quickly turned to enthusiasm.

"This is huge! Don't you see how huge this is?"

"We often considered that it might have had some bearing on your mother's state of mind but it's hardly going to change anything." Sheila replied defensively.

"You said she just walked out before I got back from my sleepover."

"Yes, she did."

"You also said she would never have left me."

Brenda jumped in quickly.

"She wouldn't have. I know that for a fact. She intended to be back before morning. I'd stake my life on that."

"My dad was already dead though. So, she couldn't have met him and run away."

Sheila and Brenda exchanged a glance.

Frankie looked from one to the other.

"You think my dad saw her leave to find him and followed her in a rage, don't you?"

"Well, either that or she ran off with a dead man!" Sheila laughed.

No-one laughed with her.

Sheila frowned.

Frankie and Brenda made eye contact in silence.

A sudden chill entered the room as three minds simultaneously allowed the possibility some airtime.

"It's ridiculous." Brenda smiled.

Sheila and Frankie both smiled back.

The ridiculous suggestion had been suitably put to bed but it had left a distinct and deep footprint on each of them. The theory that Frank had somehow lured her away, and kept her there. A prisoner.

Frankie continued her education, skiving needlecraft and cookery to study for physics and chemistry, and gained remarkable grades in her carefully selected subjects.

She had made the decision to become a psychologist. She had secretly made the decision to become a parapsychologist.

Somehow, she was going to find out what happened to her mother on the night of her sleepover.

Neither Sheila nor Brenda suspected that many of her visits to friend's houses were fictitious. Many were not but, on the occasions when they were invented, she was deep in the wood in the place Brenda had taken her. In her mother's thinking place. In the place she felt most likely to find that illusive connection of one mind to another.

She tried desperately to do everything in the books she'd read. To relax. To allow her thoughts of her mother to flow through her. To reach out to that image.

Sometimes she felt closer to something, but it still felt so far away that reaching for it felt impossible.

Always, she would drudge back home with a heavy heart and the need to invent hilarious stories about the fun time she'd had at the friend's house whose name had often escaped her.

Very little changed in her years at secondary school.

Her friends hooked up with boyfriends leaving her temporarily adrift but soon they returned with anger and hatred in their hearts. She would console them, restore their self-esteem and wait for the next disastrous liaison to sweep them away again.

But her reluctance to interact in any way with the opposite sex was causing Brenda as much concern as her dogged obsession with mind-reading and the paranormal.

She collected newspaper cuttings of strange events around the world. Of children who had claimed to be reincarnated and held memories of previous families, of strange connections between twins who claimed to feel the pain of the other, of people who had suffered complete memory loss and returned years later with it fully restored.

Brenda would move the scrapbooks back and forth as she cleaned Frankie's room and each time she flipped one open, her heart would skip a beat. Something was wrong here. Very wrong.

The long overdue conversation came when the time arrived for Frankie to pick her subjects for the final exams.

"What's wrong with science?" Frankie asked. "I could understand it if you were objecting to art, music and PE!"

"There's nothing wrong with the sciences. Nothing at all," Brenda replied, "but a career is a very important choice, and it has to be a choice that fills you with happiness. Happiness and joy."

"But you know how much I'm into science. You know that!"

"Come and sit down for a minute, Frankie." Brenda patted the sofa beside her invitingly.

Frankie folded her arms and slumped into the empty space.

"We have one life Frankie. Just one. You need to do everything you can to make every moment as wonderful as it can be. I know that your enthusiasm for science is powerful but I think it is coming from a place that won't make you happy."

"I don't know what you're talking about!"

"I think you do. I've seen so many wasted lives Frankie. Lives wasted because of a goal. An obsession or a promise and I don't want to witness another."

"What lives? What promises? You're not making any sense!"

"I watched your Grandad. You probably don't even remember him."

"I do. He was always grumpy. He died in our house."

"Yes, he did. You're right, he was miserable and that's because he made himself a promise to spend his entire life devoted to loving your Grandma, who was already dead."

"That's stupid. You can't love a dead person."

"That's right. You can love the memory of them and if you believe they are still out there somewhere, watching over you then the only thing you can do for them is to be happy. That's what they would want to see. Or, if they are away somewhere, that's what they would want to come back to. To know that the person they love is living their best life."

"You're talking about mummy, aren't you?"

"Yes I am. She would be heart-broken to find that her little girl had wasted her life obsessing over her disappearance. That's how I'd feel. Wouldn't you?"

"But when you really, really love someone, that's how you show it. By never giving up."

"No Frankie. You don't. Look at your dad. He wouldn't give up on your mummy and look where it got him! If you love someone. Really love someone then the way to show it is to let them go. Let them live their own best life. Don't waste your own by trying to change what can't be changed."

Frankie didn't reply.

They sat in silence for almost a minute before Brenda realised that Frankie was silently crying.

"Oh Frankie. What is it?"

"I don't think I have a best life to live."

"Why would you say that?"

"Because it's true. I'm never going to have a family of my own or be a mummy to anyone. I'm never going to take my daughter to school like mummy did with me or make special teas or any of that."

"Of course you will. Why do you think that?"

Frankie gave a little sob before replying.

"Because I don't like boys."

Brenda pulled her close and smiled.

"That will change. Over time that will change Frankie. You'll see and you're going to have a wonderful husband and lots of wonderful children someday."

Frankie put her arms around Brenda's waist and squeezed so tightly Brenda could barely breathe.

"But what if it doesn't change. What if I always feel like this?"

"Then there are other ways to do all those things. To look after children and be a huge part of their lives. You could be a teacher and that's like being a mum to hundreds of children. Look at me! I can't ever have a child of my own but I feel like a mum."

Brenda felt the grip loosen and as she raked back Frankie's hair from her tear-stained face she saw the glimmer of acceptance in Frankie's eyes.

"You *are* a mum." She said firmly. "You're *my* mum."

Brenda felt the warmth rise inside her. Her words had not fallen on deaf ears and as she continued to hold Frankie in her arms, she could almost feel the relief melt into her young body.

Frankie had been released from the burden of her quest to find her missing mother and also her fear of needing a man and with that relief a new Frankie had been born.

She dropped the sciences and selected the generic subjects more fitting to the career of a junior-school teacher.

Chapter 14

Unlike Frankie, both Brenda and Sheila were far from content with the prospect of a life of celibacy.

It had been four years since Brian's incarceration and neither had felt the arms of a man around them since that terrible day of his arrest.

Brenda was approaching her 30th birthday and working in the doctor's surgery on reception and Sheila was now in the twilight years of her fifties, as the decade of the eighties drew to a close.

Often, she would pass by the old garage where the sign 'Gilbert and Son' was tatty and peeling but still visible. Brian's father had passed away three years after his son's trial, but he'd been determined to keep it 'moth-balled' so that there was at least a job to come back to and his mother was honouring that decision.

The dilapidated building now stood derelict like an abandoned shop in a ghost-town. Yet another haunting for Brenda to endure and another burden for her guilt-ridden conscience. No-one had ever said it out loud, but she knew that Charlie Gilbert had given up on life after the heartbreak of his son's fate. There had been occasions when she had passed Jean on the street and been met with a cordial nod which caused that guilt to sting her again. The woman possessed more composure and forgiveness than she would ever have done in her shoes. Between herself and Mealy they had totally destroyed that woman's life. They had used her son shamefully. Tricked her into believing she had a grandchild and then instigated his arrest and conviction.

Often, Brenda would approach that empty forecourt and still imagine the scattered cars in various stages of repair. The cheeky banter and smiling faces emerging from that dirty little office. Brian and Charlie laughing, in their greasy overalls flicking one another with oily rags or playfully pushing and shoving. Those were the happy days. The lives she had murdered more cruelly than Brian murdered Frank!

Now there seemed to be nothing left other than her pitiful empty life and the years were passing her by.

"I don't want to spend the rest of my life alone as a sad old spinster." Brenda announced on an evening when Frankie had stayed over at a friend's house to study for a test.

"Frankie's going to be here for quite a few more years!" Sheila laughed. "She's got GCSE's then A levels, then university. You're not going to be alone for a long time yet! I'm not planning on popping my clogs any time soon either!"

"You know what I mean." Brenda huffed.

Sheila emptied the remains of her glass of wine down her throat and smiled.

"Yes, I know exactly what you mean. Neither of us have had a fulfilling sex life have we? Apart from your early bed-hopping years, you had Brian for what? Five years?"

"If that!"

"And apart from my own campervan hopping days I had Tom for a week and Barry for about a decade. It all adds up to a pathetic love-life doesn't it? Perhaps it's time we did something about it and got ourselves some new glad rags!"

Brenda spurted her mouthful of wine into the air!

"Don't you think we're a bit old to be going out on the town in high heels and skimpy tops!"

Sheila grinned. "Well, *you* might be, but I've got a few miles left in my engine!"

Brenda flopped onto the sofa and laughed out her heartache for the wasted years, the lonely nights, and the void in her life where her sister had once lived, where her mother and father had once lived and where her own family would never live.

It had been a drunken conversation, but it had also been an awakening. A silent pact had been made for the two sad spinsters to set off in search of love again.

For the next few years, as Frankie became engrossed in her education and girlfriends, Sheila and Brenda were engrossed in the possibility of finding a man to share their respective beds.

Sheila's hunting ground was the community centre and local working men's club where she met several available older men. All of them widowed and most of them still grieving. Her evenings had mostly been spent listening to their memories of wonderful wives who no longer lived anywhere other than in their over-crammed hearts. There was no room for her. Sometimes she would receive an appeasing, half-heated apologetic kiss and on one occasion she found herself the victim of nothing other than pent-up sexual frustration but nothing even close to love.

Brenda's experience had been very different but equally catastrophic. Her stunning good looks had always attracted a stream of men into the surgery with pathetic excuses to strike up a conversation but now she started to engage with them. The result was a succession of cheating husbands or bitter divorcees. Sex was very much on the agenda but thankfully, she could read between the lines. Their promises of leaving unsuspecting wives fell on deaf ears and so did their stories of the bitches they had walked out on. None of the liaisons lasted more than a couple of dates and none of them resulted in any intimacy.

Her co-worker shook her head and chuckled in amusement at her latest narrow escape from a divorcee who had taken Brenda on a date to stalk his ex-wife!

"Most of these men are far too old for you, Brenda! You need to be looking a decade younger!" Annette laughed.

"A toyboy? No thanks!"

"Well, someone nearer your own age. You're still young. If you were a few years younger, I'd suggest my son!"

Brenda looked Annette up and down for a second and then frowned.

"Surely, your son is a child?"

"Malcolm's twenty actually but I think you're probably needing someone with an established career or at least a bit of money behind them. You'd make a handsome couple though."

"He's only five years older than my daughter!" Brenda squealed. I don't need another child to look after!"

Annette pretended to look disappointed and then grinned.

"I kinda' liked the idea of us becoming family and imagine how gorgeous my grandchildren would be!"

Brenda felt flattered. She'd only ever thought of Anette as a colleague but clearly the woman considered her a friend. She made a mental note to try harder to reciprocate that friendship and made a stronger mental note to stop trying to find a new man.

There were a few more half-hearted efforts by both Sheila and Brenda which they aptly named the 'death-throws of dating'. It was exhausting, consistently disappointing and severely depressing.

During those short years of discontent, Sheila found herself mischievously re-arranging Barry's gnomes while he was out and constantly checking his washing line for female clothing.

Brenda found herself sleeping on Brian's side of the bed and stroking old photographs of summer holidays where he held little Frankie akimbo on the beach or, with his arm around both of them when Frankie was about nine. Those were the days she yearned for. Even living under the cloud of her missing sister, those were the days she had been the happiest but now there was no happiness on any horizon.

Frankie left for university and Brenda was finding it difficult to cope. The time had come far too quickly. Much faster than Sheila had promised.

The reconvening of the spinster duo didn't take place until the night before Frankie's graduation.

They were sitting in the same room with a similar bottle of wine when Sheila opened the conversation.

"Well, that was a crap idea, wasn't it?"

"What was?"

"That bloody scavenger hunt for a good man! There aren't any!"

It took several seconds for Brenda to catch on.

"You're talking about the night we decided not to be sad old spinsters!"

"Yep. It was a crap idea! I'd rather have spent those nights with you or Frankie than being pawed and cried on by a string of sweaty nitwits!"

Brenda laughed out loud as Sheila poured herself a second glass.

"I keep sneaking round to Barry's you know."

"You don't!"

"I do." Sheila's eyes widened. "I'm like a stalking teenager. I re-arrange his gnomes. I put the man gnome on top of the woman once!"

Brenda laughed and then her heart sank.

"I've got a post-office box."

"Why? What for?"

Brenda topped up her a glass and sat down on the chair opposite.

Sheila studied the woman she'd raised, and her heart sank too.

Before her, this beautiful blonde woman with her perfect hour-glass figure and huge heart had missed the life she deserved. The burden Amelia had bestowed on her, had stolen her youth. The man she would have married had she not been so invested in her sister's debris. The children she might have adopted with the man who would have loved her completely.

"I use the box to receive letters from Brian." She confessed.

"You're in contact with him?"

"Yes, I got back in contact last year, but I didn't want his letters dropping on the mat with a prison stamp on them. I don't want Frankie to think I've betrayed her."

"Perhaps you should talk to her?"

"No. She seems settled and focussed. I'm not going to do anything to risk changing that. She still thinks it's possible that he killed her mummy and if she knew I was in contact with him that would be the worst kind of betrayal."

"What about you? What do you believe?"

"It's not what I believe, it's what I know. Brian isn't capable of ever hurting Amelia."

"Maybe not back then. On the night he hit Frank but on the night she walked out. Well, that was totally different."

"What do you mean?"

"I mean that when she came back for those few hours everything had changed. He already knew she'd chosen Frank the year before and since then, he'd changed too."

"Changed how?"

"He'd fallen in love with you! You must know that? He was head over heels in love with you and now suddenly, his unfaithful wife was back! Wanting to slip back into her role as Frankie's mum. A role that was already taken. He didn't want her back. You must see that. He only wanted you and Frankie! Then, when she went out again, looking for Frank, well….."

"You think he killed her?"

"I think it's possible. Understandable even."

"But he loved Amelia!"

"Once, maybe but on that night he didn't. He loved you!"

Brenda was reeling.

She stared at that round face that had been her anchor, her compass and her refuge for most of her life. The face that had somehow become entangled with this family when she was a young, pretty woman who fell in love with a boy and remained in love with the man he became. In love with her father until the very end.

The face now lined with the heartache she'd endured and barely recognisable from the photographs she smiled back from, as a doll-faced, long-haired hippy with a ring of flowers around her head as she made the sign of peace at the camera. Her hipster jeans revealing a smooth, toned midriff and gently sloping hips. She had been such a pretty young thing and now she sat in that chair, wrinkled and bloated and that pretty face was barely recognisable.

It seemed suddenly ironic that the one photograph Brenda had ever seen of Sheila's younger days was that one. The one outside a campervan at some festival or other as she made that sign of peace with her fingers. It was the most fitting photograph of Sheila that depicted her whole being. A woman of peace. A woman of conscience and truths. Sheila's words were always worth listening to.

Suddenly she was remembering how annoyed Brian had been when she'd had to move back out of the marital bed to hide their affair from Amelia.

How irritated he'd seemed by her sudden reappearance.

In all her recent letters from Brian, never once had he shown any affection for Amelia, nor had he seemed perplexed at her unexplained absence.

She turned her face away from Sheila and tried to process what it meant to her if Sheila was right.

Her love for Brian had never diminished. Brian was the only man who had ever felt like home. The only man who filled her with such contentment and joy. Having him and Frankie in her life as a family had given her the most wonderful years of her life but what if he really had killed her sister. Her Mealy!

It felt impossible to choose!

The bond between two lovers versus the bond between siblings.

The options were totally incomparable. It was like choosing between food and air.

The next day, Brenda and Sheila stood side by side as Frankie's remaining, long-suffering but very proud parents as she threw her cap into the air and drank a glass of bubbly with her classmates.

It felt like another milestone.

The turning of another page.

Brenda wrote her final letter to Brian without sharing her new suspicions but informing him that she was giving up the post office box number due to the guilt she'd been feeling. She wished him well and broke all communication.

Sheila, however, continued to re-arrange Barry's gnomes and check the garments on his washing line.

Both women had tried to read between the lines of Frankie's letters from university. Was she eating? Was she struggling with her studies? Was she making friends? More importantly, did she have a boyfriend?

She'd returned home often and seemed happy and excited about becoming a teacher and collected quotations of what it meant to be remembered in the life of a child. The quotations were always recorded in an old book meant for autographs and kept at home in her room. The quotations she collected were scribbled on bits of paper stuffed into her bag until she could sit in her room and record them meticulously in her book.

To Benda, it seemed like a positive attitude. She was finally putting all her energy into something worthwhile, but Sheila was silently harbouring concerns she'd decided to keep to herself for the time being.

Sheila had noticed the absence of any boys anywhere near Frankie on the photographs of university nights out. Many of the girls had an arm around a boy but Frankie was always standing alone or joined onto a couple for the shot.

But now she was coming back home and starting to enquire about positions in schools around Rochdale. It was clearly her intention to keep her wings firmly by her side and settle back in her hometown. A decision which put a huge smile on Brenda's face and a huge frown on Sheila's.

"I don't know what you're so worried about Sheila." Brenda snapped. "It'll be great to have her working around here. She'll probably meet a local boy and settle down right here where we can watch her family grow."

Sheila couldn't argue with the theory, but her intuition was already arguing against the likelihood of Frankie, now twenty-two, ever leaving the safety Cherry Blossom House.

She was, however, welcomed with open arms by both women as they unburdened her of her cases and boxes and dragged them up to her room.

They proudly spread the news among the neighbours of her new position at the junior school and as the first year passed, they revelled in the feedback from parents. Tales of children who had never been so happy to skip off to school, to join after school activities and to excel where previously they had been falling behind.

As a new term started, Brenda had been commended for her dedication and engagement with the children in her care.

It was during this year of tentative normality that Sheila reported a few strange phone calls.

"That's three times this week that I've picked up the phone and been hung up on! Someone's playing pranks on us!"

"The same thing's been happening to me!" Frankie called from the kitchen. "Could just be kids messing around."

Brenda didn't comment. It hadn't happened to her, and she was wondering if someone was waiting until they heard her own voice before speaking.

Someone who didn't want to be heard by anyone else!

Chapter 15

Brenda spent the next week keeping as close as she could to the hallway, and she didn't have to wait long for the mystery to be solved.

Sheila was upstairs and Frankie was at work when she picked up the receiver and whispered hello.

"Ah! It's you at last." Came the voice that caused her heart to skip a beat.

"Brian! Have you been released?"

"Yeah. Well, I'm out on parole anyway. I wasn't sure if you'd want to hear from me, or if you might be ex-directory!"

"How could you think that! Of course, I want to hear from you! I would have continued writing but.."

"I know, I know. You don't need to explain. Do you want to meet up for a coffee and a chat at some point?"

Brenda's heart was already pounding. There was nothing she wanted more but she needed to keep her cool.

"Yes, why not? I'd need to be discreet though."

"Of course. No-one wants to be seen with a murderer!"

"I didn't mean that!"

"I'm kidding. I know what you meant. Are you free this afternoon?"

"I could be."

"Do you drive?"

"I do."

"Got a car?"

"I have."

Brian laughed.

"Got a husband?"

Brenda felt the impact of his question. He wanted to know if there was still a chance for them.

"No husband. No boyfriend." She replied excitedly.

"I hear there's a new posh country pub a couple of miles up the Manchester Road. Perhaps we could meet there at say, one?"

"Sounds good. I'll see you in a bit then."

"Who was that?" Sheila's voice caused her to jump.

"What are you doing creeping around? You scared the life out of me!"

"I heard your tone, and I was curious as to who was causing you to behave like an excited child!"

Brenda turned to face her with the intention of either telling her to mind her business or lying, but as her eyes met Sheila's she was sunk. Sheila knew she was up to something.

"I was just talking to someone I quite like."

Sheila frowned and Brenda blushed instantly.

"Look, Brenda. You're not a child. You don't need to explain anything to me. Whatever it is I'm sure I'll find out soon enough and when I do I'll either be here to share the joy of it or here to pick up the pieces."

As Brenda went upstairs to get ready, she remembered the day Sheila came into their lives and the day she'd told Amelia that she believed their mother had sent her to look after them. She had never really believed that, but she did believe that if her mother had any influence over who might step in and take her place, she couldn't have chosen any better than the woman who was now boiling the kettle downstairs.

An hour later she was on her way to meet the man she hadn't been alone with since the morning she kissed him goodbye as he left for work over a decade ago.

She chose to wear jeans with heels and a pink mohair sweater as there was still a nip in the air as spring had not yet given way to summer. She'd scrunched her hair with mousse to accentuate the waves and allowed them to fall loosely against the pink background of her shoulders. She'd taken care with her makeup. Subtle shades of beige eyeshadow, no liner and a peach lipstick.

She didn't want him to think she was regarding this as a date.

As she pulled up, he was already seated at a wooden table in the garden. He watched her glance in the mirror before flicking her hair back and stepping out onto the gravel in her flimsy heels. He smiled instantly. Brenda was regarding this as a date.

He rose to his feet as she approached and grinned.

"I took the liberty of ordering you a coffee." He greeted.

She smiled back. "Is it cold?"

He quickly picked up on the inference.

"I haven't been sat here waiting for hours you know! No, it isn't cold."

She sat down, took a sip and then grinned. "It's stone cold!"

"I know."

No ice was broken because none had ever formed.

He reached for her hand, and she allowed him to take it. Then they chatted for over an hour without ordering anything else.

He told her about the courses he'd taken in prison and how he was pretty well informed about new engine technology and how he wanted to get the old garage up and running again.

She told him about Frankie's career and how well she was doing and before long the catch-up was complete. There was nothing more to report.

They sat in silence for a minute until Brian found the courage to say it.

"I never stopped loving you Bren. I've loved you since the moment you writhed those cases to my car in London and I love you still. I think I always will."

The tears choked Brenda's reply, causing him to squeeze her hand comfortingly.

She took a deep breath.

"I'm so so sorry, Brian. You have no idea how much I regret what I did to you, to us, to Frankie. A moment of sheer stupidity ruined all of us."

He placed his long finger over her lips and smiled gently. His face still bore the scars of that spotty teenager and his wiry hair was still an unruly mess, but he had never looked more inviting.

She felt his gentle touch on her lips and her heart started racing. She could remember the thrill of his attentive lovemaking, and the protection of his long arms around her body. This ungainly man was never going to turn any heads, but he would always turn hers because he was her soulmate. He was the one person who was always on her side. Always forgiving and understanding of her many flaws.

This man was her home. Her only home.

"I don't know what to do." She sighed.

"You don't have to do anything." He whispered. "I'm not asking you for anything."

She didn't reply.

The things she wanted to say were pressing against her brain, straining to be released but these were words she had no right to say. Words she didn't deserve to speak.

She kept her eyes diverted for several seconds as though that might somehow prevent him from catching a whisper of them.

When she looked back at him, his eyes were already fixed on hers with the gentle acceptance of defeat.

That look caused her heart to sink. This had not been a date or even a rendezvous to explore any options or to pick through the wreckage for some glimmer of life. This was nothing other than the closing of the door that she'd had her foot wedged into for many years.

He took her hand in his and kissed it.

She closed her eyes and allowed the touch of his lips to seep through her skin and into her soul, dissolving her restraint and releasing the desire that was scorching her heart.

"But I love you, Brian. I love you! Only you! I ache for you every minute of every day! I know I don't deserve your love but that doesn't stop me from wanting it. We had a wonderful life together. You, me and Frankie. We did, didn't we?"

He smiled. "The best."

Then she waited. Hoping for something more but he remained silent.

That silence hung in the air like a deafening siren. She couldn't believe he had nothing more to say.

"But you said you still love me? Is that true?" She asked meekly.

"You know it is."

"Even after what I did?"

He gave a little humorous huff.

"You must remember that I am not an innocent man here, Bren. I am not the victim. I did a terrible thing too. More terrible than anything you did to me, but I've accepted responsibility for it. I got what I deserved. You and Frankie were just collateral damage and that was all my fault. You keep saying that you had a moment of madness in reporting me but what about my moment of madness? I think mine trumps yours don't you!"

His words were humble, truthful and factual and they bore the tone of a person who had drawn a thick black line under the past and accepted that there was no way back. Brenda didn't possess that ability to give up on the past or on the life she craved to resurrect no matter how unrealistic it seemed.

"If you love me then I think maybe I could speak to Frankie. I know she still loves you too. I've seen her photo album and they are mostly of the two of you. The models you made for school projects, the medal she put around your neck when you won the dad's race on sports day."

"I'm sure she still has some fond memories of me, Bren and I'm sure she wants to believe I had nothing to do with her mother's disappearance, but a jury believed differently. I don't blame her for feeling how she does. I would feel the same and even with that aside, I still killed her father. Her real father."

"He meant nothing to her!" Brenda snapped. "She knows why you hit him, and she knows you didn't mean to kill him. You were fighting to keep the family you loved. Fighting for her!"

Brian sighed heavily.

"Listen Bren. If, one day, Amelia was to walk back through that door at our old house, then things might be different. I've spent years and years praying for her to come back. Cursing her for every day she didn't vindicate me of her murder. But now.... well, now I've given up on that ever happening. Perhaps she did get caught up in something related to Frank's past that accounted for her missing year. Perhaps her confusion on the day she briefly returned, was real or perhaps it was fake. Maybe she's got a new life with a new man? I've gone through every scenario I can think of, but the result is the same. She's gone and I've been labelled as her murderer. I'm not hoping for a miracle anymore."

"Can't you explain it to Frankie?"

"Bren, I love you and I love our little girl. I always will no matter how old she is, she will always be my little girl. You know that but we can't turn back the clock. This doubt, this suspicion would be at the heart of our lives, like a huge tumour and it would taint every aspect of our existence. We have to move on now, but I promise you this," he took her hand and held it tightly, "there will never be another woman in my life. I once thought I loved Amelia, but now I know that wasn't love. It was just the euphoria of being given the chance to be with a girl. I felt grateful, lucky and shocked but I didn't really feel love. Well not the kind of love I felt with you, and I don't expect or even yearn to feel that again with anyone else. That was our love. Yours and mine."

In that final speech Brenda felt all hope dissolve. She knew he was right, and she knew that she had no capability to move on any more than he did. She didn't want anyone else in her bed either, but she was just the weaker person here. She had to find the same strength he'd found. The strength to face life alone. At least she had Frankie.

No more words were spoken.

He leaned in for a gentle kiss, but her lips held his for a second too long. He knew he should pull away, but he couldn't. He slid his hand into the nape of her neck and kissed her with more feeling than he had ever kissed her before. This was his woman, his lover, his soulmate, and that final kiss would be the most tortuous, beautiful, heartbreaking moment of his life.

As Brian drove away that day, he could barely see the road for tears.

As soon as Brenda's car was out of sight, he pulled over.

His entire body ached for the woman he had just rejected, and the only salvation would be the return of another woman.

Suddenly anger rushed through his veins. He was certain Amelia was still alive somewhere and all he needed, was for her to show her face, vindicate him from her murder and give him back the family he loved.

He banged his fist on the steering wheel and cursed her for her selfishness. For her cold-hearted abandonment and her unforgivable desertion of their child.

He imagined her living her life somewhere. Happy and indifferent to their plight. She must have read of his conviction. Perhaps she was now too afraid to return after causing so much misery.

His hatred turned to frantic pleading for her to send some proof of life before it was too late.

He got out of the car and threw out his arms with his face to the sky and screamed at the universe in desperation and hope that she would somehow hear his voice and take pity on him.

"Amelia! Where the hell are you?"

Chapter 16

Sheila was reading the newspaper when Brenda arrived home.

"How is he?" She asked without looking up.

"How's who?"

Sheila simply peered over her spectacles with the same knowing look she used to make when they were children.

"How did you know?"

"I heard he was out a couple of weeks ago, then the silent phone calls and then you, sneaking out looking like that! I'd hardly need to be Sherlock Holmes."

"Well, to answer your question. He's ok."

"And you?"

Sheila had done it again! Infiltrated her armour.

"I think I'm alright." She replied tentatively as though checking. "I think it's exactly what I needed to move on." Her second statement was less convincing, even to herself. It was true that she felt better but her ability to move on was still in doubt.

Sheila unravelled her grey, wiry topknot and let it fall to her shoulders before unceremoniously re-capturing it and securing it back on top of her head. Sheila was not the only one who had learned to read the other. Brenda knew this was Sheila's way of allowing herself some thinking time. The thing she did to create a small interruption in which she could mull something over.

"Did he say he wanted to be free of you now then?"

"No. Not exactly."

"I thought not." Sheila sighed as she picked up her paper again. "This isn't over."

She gave the paper a shake to straighten it and then spoke in a whisper.

"I'm not sure it ever will be."

Brenda knew better than to challenge her. There was no point because she would be lying anyway, and Sheila would know it.

The details of that meeting between Brenda and Brian were never discussed again but there was a cordial, silent acknowledgement between Sheila and Brenda. The knowledge that despite their commitment to stay away from each other, Brenda and Brian were still very much in love.

She watched Brenda draw a thick line under it and channel all her energy and emotion back towards her remaining family. This tiny, all female family of three.

The years passed by in a gentle air of feigned contentment, but Sheila was feeling unsettled by the satisfied ambience in that house. That over emphasized sense of gratification that Frankie had achieved her goal in life. That, for her, this was it. Her vocation had become her entire life, and no-one seemed to be mentioning the fact that she never strayed from the very narrow path between the school and that house.

The years were speeding by with no sign of a boyfriend, no hint of her planning to get a place of her own and no hint of any fear that life was quickly passing her by.

"She's going to make headmistress." Brenda smiled after returning from Brenda's room with an empty tray. "She's still working up there.! When I was at school the teachers left at four and didn't seem to do anything until the next day! Have you noticed how much of her own time she puts in?"

"Yes, I have." Sheila replied blandly. "She seems to do nothing else."

"You say that, like it's a bad thing!"

"Well, isn't it? All work and no play, and all that? She's already well into her thirties without a boyfriend in sight Bren! What about her own life? Her own family?"

"But haven't you noticed how happy and contented she is? Those kids are like one huge family, and she loves it.!"

Sheila didn't want to pour cold water onto Brenda's pathetic little flame of joy, so she simply smiled and nodded that she had indeed noticed.

She'd noticed much more than the presumed state of happiness. She'd noticed how Frankie's heels were getting lower and her necklines were getting higher. That most of her new clothes were grey suits and the hair that used to cascade down her back like a gorgeous black curtain was now cruelly captured in a tight bun at the nape of her neck. She seemed to be skipping a stage of her life and heading straight into middle age!

Sheila felt the need to drop a subtle hint.

"Soon we'll be the three old spinsters!" She laughed.

Brenda huffed her indignation and took the tray to the kitchen.

She collected her coat from the hallway and called back haughtily.

"I'm going into town for a bit."

Sheila smiled in recognition that she'd taken the bait.

Brenda slammed the door and strode down the path. She needed a bit of thinking time to consider Sheila's words and the best way to do that wasn't really to go shopping but it was, however, the best way to prove the woman wrong.

The fact that Frankie had hit her thirties had caused Brenda's heart to sink. Her child-bearing years were limited! Time was running out.

A few minutes ago, she'd felt content with life, but Sheila's words had given her a devastating wake-up call. Frankie's youth had been slipping away and so had her own. Three spinsters stuck in a routine where neither romance nor passion existed and suddenly everything felt very urgent.

She'd spent years revelling in Frankie's teaching success with nothing other than an occasional, pathetic strut in front of Brian's garage to appease her lust for male attention.

The days when she had shamefully 'dressed to kill', driven back across town to park at the end of the street, and walked seductively over his forecourt. She knew now that it hadn't been a quest to torment him but a desperate attempt not to be forgotten. This forbidden desire was the only morsel of sexuality she had left and her fear that the tiny flame that still burned between them might flicker out completely drove her to desperate measures.

Sheila's words had hit her right in the stomach - the three old spinsters!

Frankie would never be left on any shelf if she had anything to do with it! She had a plan!

She wasn't the only one with a reluctant fledgling still refusing to leave the nest. The boy her colleague had once tried to pair her off with was also refusing to budge. She couldn't believe she hadn't thought of it before!

She listened to the poor woman every day. Desperately trying to prevent her chance of becoming a grandma slip away and suddenly it all seemed so perfectly obvious.

She intended to buy Frankie a sexy new dress and invite Anette and her husband over to dinner with their, good-looking son, Malcolm who was now a design engineer.

It was a perfect match.

She returned home and stashed her purchase in her room until Frankie disappeared to plan her lessons.

Sheila stared at the dress Brenda was holding.

"You're kidding!"

"What's wrong with it!"

"What's right with it!" Sheila bellowed. "It looks like something a lap-dancer would wear! Honestly Brenda, sometimes I worry about your judgment. It's flipping February. It's freezing and that dress has got 'set-up' written all over it! The poor man would be terrified if Frankie walked in wearing that!"

Brenda felt her face flush.

The low-cut satin mini dress in electric blue was definitely more suited to a nightclub than a family dinner.

Sheila was right.... Again!

She quietly folded it and returned it to the bag.

Sheila patted her hand comfortingly and smiled.

"Just let her be herself. She's a beautiful young woman and any man is going to be enchanted. Especially if she isn't thrusting her breasts in his face!"

Brenda laughed out loud. Sheila always managed to bring out the best in her.

"What are you two laughing at?" Frankie asked disinterestedly as she strolled through the door and switched on the tv.

"Nothing much." Sheila replied. "Your mum's invited her work friend over for dinner tomorrow night because the poor woman seems to regard her as her best friend."

"What's wrong with that?" Frankie frowned as she switched channels.

"Nothing, except your mum had hardly noticed her after years of working together!"

Brenda sighed and smiled at Sheila for the improvised explanation.

"I was hoping you'd join us?" Brenda added.

"Suppose I have to, if I want to get fed tomorrow. Never known you to host a dinner party before! Has the poor woman ever tasted your cooking!"

Brenda didn't reply.

Frankie was already engrossed in her programme, but the task had been accomplished so she discreetly collected the bag containing the slutty dress and took it up to her room.

Once inside, she locked the door and slipped it on.

She swept up her long blonde hair with her hands provocatively and imagined Brian lying on the bed watching her.

He would have loved it!

It was a moment of revelation for Brenda.

As she strutted sexily back and forth in that dress two facts became blatantly clear.

Firstly, she was still a very curvy, sexy and provocative woman and secondly, there was only one man in the entire world she wanted to impress or arouse and that was Brian!

She allowed her hair to fall back onto her shoulders and flopped onto the bed.

Where are you? –Part 2   Three Hours

Staring up at the ceiling, she aimed all her hatred once again at the woman who had allowed her duty for justice to steal her happiness. The stupid former self who had kissed the love of her life goodbye and marched proudly to the police station with the bomb that would destroy his world, her own world, and the world of their adopted daughter.

She wanted to scream!

She ripped out a chunk of her own hair, tore of the dress and threw it in the bin along with her dreams.

No justice had been done here!

Her only chance of ever feeling Brian in her arms again would be if Amelia walked back through that door or if Frankie left home, had a family, and emigrated!

The second option seemed to be the most likely of the two.

Downstairs, Sheila was making a list of the things she needed to produce the dinner party Brenda would otherwise make a mess of.

She glanced at Frankie sitting in her pyjamas with her feet on the footstool chomping crisps and laughing at some American comedy show with canned laughter.

This wasn't living. Not for any of them.

Something needed to change.

She returned to her shopping list and allowed herself to believe for a moment that a dinner party would at least inject something new into their existence.

The following day was a Saturday and Sheila spent it preparing the three courses that could be refrigerated and finished off later.

Unlike the missing dress, her menu was more fitting to the time of year with homemade soup, chicken and mushroom stroganoff and her own special toffee pudding.

Brenda was setting the table when Frankie noticed the number of places.

"Why have you set six places?"

"Oh, they asked if they could bring their son along." Brenda replied in the most nonchalant voice she could muster.

Frankie rolled her eyes. "Haven't they heard of babysitters?"

Brenda didn't correct her.

"Are you going to get ready then?"

"Yes, I'm on my way. Don't worry, I won't come to your dinner party in my PJ's." She assured comically.

Frankie was still getting ready when she heard the guests arrive. The voice of a man and a woman, then Brenda's and a cordial welcome from Sheila. She assumed the son had been ushered in the direction of the television.

She'd acted like the whole thing was an inconvenience but secretly, Frankie had been looking forward to having an excuse to make some effort.

She captured her hair, smoothed it with hair gloss and twisted it over one shoulder before securing it with a pretty jewelled clasp. She slipped on her skintight jeans and picked out a baby blue silk ruffle blouse that followed her curves perfectly and then she set to work on her make-up. She shaped her brows with eye shadow, coloured her eyelids with layers of subtle browns and then added a flourish of liner before curling her lashes with dark mascara. She finished the job with peach lip-gloss and stood back to appraise the result.

An involuntary smile spread across her face.

She was a beautiful woman.

She made her way downstairs to join the gathering in the living room and as she entered, five heads turned. Five adults!

She recognised Annette from Brenda's description and assumed the small, worried looking man beside her was her husband. The little boy she'd expected had however, been replaced by a very handsome man who smiled warmly before returning to the conversation he was having with Sheila.

Frankie picked up the remaining glass of wine from the tray and smiled back before moving to Brenda's side.

"Well mum. I can see why they didn't need a babysitter!" She whispered.

"I thought you might not come down if I told you." Brenda whispered back.

"You were probably right." Frankie smiled.

As they took their places at the dinner table, Brenda and Sheila instantly took the ends of the table, leaving the others to sit in closer proximity.

Frankie found herself seated directly opposite Malcom.

As she refilled her glass, she offered to do the same for him, but he placed his hand over it.

"Not for me thanks. I'm driving." He smiled. "I think I've only been invited as the chauffeur to be honest."

She looked back at him, but he'd already turned away to continue his conversation with Sheila about meditation.

Frankie felt suddenly offended. She had no intention of looking for romance, but this man seemed to be totally unaffected by her presence and it irritated her.

Even without makeup and wearing her baggy jumpers she managed to turn heads on the weekends, but this particular man seemed totally immune to her charms.

At the end of the main course, which he ate greedily, Brenda suggested they take a break and go back into the living room before serving dessert.

Frankie made sure she entered directly behind Malcolm so she could sit beside this rather intriguing person. It crossed her mind that he might be a player. The kind to act cool and disinterested. The kind to make a woman feel unwanted, rejected and desperate for validation. If that was his game, then he seemed to be winning.

She sat beside him and tried to strike up a conversation about his job.

He took a gulp of his can of coke and then frowned.

"You're not interested in my job any more than I'm interested in yours." He grinned. "This is obviously a set-up. We seem to be the sad problem children incapable of finding a mate on our own."

Frankie instantly warmed to him.

"You're right. Perhaps we should play along with it?"

"Good idea! Why don't I take you for a drive or something. That is, unless you'd rather stay for dessert?"

"Nope."

"Well then, grab your coat, you've pulled!" He laughed.

"We're going out for a bit." Frankie announced.

Several pairs of eyes exchanged various glances and as they headed for the door four smiles lit up four faces.

"Shall I put my arm around you?" Malcolm whispered.

"In for a penny…" Frankie replied.

They walked to the car with arms around each other without looking back to watch the four wide-eyed faces at the window.

Malcom opened the passenger seat for her and then plonked himself in the driving seat and laughed.

"Where to?" He asked as he started the engine.

"I don't mind."

"I know of a place a few miles away where we could grab a knickerbocker glory?"

"Sounds perfect." She replied as she studied his face for the first time.

Malcolm's sandy-blonde hair had been fiercely gelled to control the stubborn waves that were already re-forming. His face was almost pretty. Almond shaped green eyes, delicate pink lips and a smooth light complexion with a sprinkling of small freckles. The only masculine feature was his jawline.

He seemed to notice her attention and glanced her way.

She quickly averted her stare but not before being stung by those vivid green eyes. He was a very attractive man.

"So, what's your excuse for refusing to follow life's depicted path?"

Frankie shrugged, thought for a moment, and then frowned.

"I think it's less painful for everyone if we all keep ourselves to ourselves."

Malcolm laughed out loud.

"I think the human race would very quickly become extinct!"

"What I mean is, that in my experience, for every couple who are happily in love, there is always a third person paying the price."

"I don't understand."

"The woman sat opposite my mum, for instance."

"Sheila?"

"Yes. Sheila. She lived her life aching for my grandad who married my grandma when he was really in love with her. Duty of an unborn child! Then there's my dad, Brian, who went to prison because my real mum, Amelia, was already in love with someone else. Not to mention Barry who was the third wheel to Sheila's affair with Grandad."

"Wow. That's quite a mess."

"Exactly. So many wasted lives. Love hurts and destroys as many people as it manages to elate. It's less painful not to get involved."

"That's one way of looking at it, I suppose."

She tried to assess his opinion on her theory, but his faint smile gave nothing away, so she decided to give him the same grilling.

"What about you then? What's your excuse for sitting on the shelf until your bum gets splinters?"

He grinned and then shook his head.

"It's far too complicated to explain."

"Coward!"

"You've probably hit the nail on the head there. I am a coward. Definitely."

"Afraid of love?"

"Not exactly but maybe I'll explain one day."

"You're talking like we are going to see more of each other!"

"There are worse ways to spend an evening!" He laughed.

She gave him a playful punch and then changed the subject.

They chatted for hours over those knickerbocker glory's about their careers and hobbies until they considered it was way past their parents' bedtime.

As they got out of the car and headed back towards the door Malcolm grinned.

"I think we're being watched."

"I'm sure of it."

He quickly slid his arm into the small of her back and pulled her towards him for a kiss.

Frankie was taken by surprise but didn't resist.

He released her after a few seconds and then grinned again. "That'll fool 'em!"

She concurred with a half-smile, but her self-esteem had just been lifted to a great height and then dropped on the floor again. Secretly she had been hoping his desire was real.

As they entered the house, they could feel the tangible excitement of hopeful parents. Self-satisfied faces stricken by erasable smiles, as images of cots and gurgling babies danced in their heads, but Frankie was still feeling something else entirely. She was feeling hurt. Already the collateral damage of an encounter with romance.

As she got into her solitary bed that night, she allowed the events of the evening to mull over.

The evening had been a revelation.

She didn't want to live the lonely life of a childless spinster, but she had no intention of becoming another victim of unrequited love.

She now knew exactly what she wanted from life and exactly how she was going to get it.

Chapter 17

Within a month of that dinner party Brenda and Annette formed a new alliance.

Self-satisfied nods and wry smiles were exchanged frequently when they compared notes to find that Malcolm and Frankie were always out on the same evenings.

"I don't know why they just don't admit it!" Annette shook her head in frustration after removing her headscarf and stuffing it into her handbag.

Brenda hated the way Annette had accepted the freefall into old age. They were both heading for the big six zero, but this woman was doing nothing to slow the process down. She was a constant reminder of what was to come, and that headscarf was definitely leading the way!

Brenda, however, had her foot firmly on the brake! She was still refusing to replace her 'hold-ups' with tights or to cut off her long blonde tresses which were now tinted to disguise the grey. Her wardrobe still consisted of tight jeans and sweaters, pencil skirts and silk blouses, trainers and heels. There were no slacks, flatties, A-line skirts, or headscarves in sight!

She still had a beauty routine involving expensive creams, UV protectors, a strict diet, and an even stricter exercise routine. Annette however seemed to take no interest in her physical appearance. Her face was always naked and dry. The lines deep and unconcealed and her eyebrows were now invisible. She was overweight and all her clothes seemed to be the same, apart from the colours. Baggy blouses with elastic necklines, nylon slacks or patterned floppy skirts, black flat shoes, or leather flat sandals.

Brenda would often look her up and down and pity her but there was something about Annette that she couldn't pity because it was something she envied.

Annette's hideous body, pensioner's perm and wrinkled face radiated undeniable joy and happiness. This was a woman who no longer needed visual approval or physical validation. Her contentment beamed from within.

Unlike Brenda, this woman was at peace with life. This woman slept with a man in her bed.

"What time did Malcolm get in?" She asked.

"Eleven." Annette smiled. "Frankie?"

"Ten thirty. He must have dropped her off up the road again."

Whilst the two women seemed content to play the game, Sheila was irritated by the whole thing.

"Why don't you just tell her that you know about them instead of whispering about it?" She snapped at Brenda one evening after Annette had reported a discrepancy in their timings. "The poor man probably just called in on a friend on his way home or something!"

"Well, I hope he's not cheating on her!" Brenda snapped. "If he is then he'll have me to deal with!"

Sheila reached out and caught Brenda by both hands.

"What's really going on here Bren?"

"Nothing."

Shela didn't need to say any more. She just cocked her head with that look on her face and Brenda crumbled as Sheila let go of her hands.

"Do you remember years ago when Mealy and I used to do those mind-reading tricks?"

"Of course, I do! You used to scare the shit out of me with it!"

"Really? I thought you said it was all just nonsense?"

"That's because I didn't want you dabbling in it all. It was unnerving and your dad asked me to snuff it out."

"So, you really knew we were onto something? It wasn't just our imaginations?"

"Yes. Of course I did, and it caused me to do a lot of research on it. Some of the things you used to say would chill me to the bone. Like the time Amelia was late home from school and it was getting dark."

"I don't remember that!"

"Well, I do. It was probably so normal to you that you didn't even realise but you told me not to worry because she'd been with a new boy from school and she was on her way home, just passing the co-op. I watched from the window and within a minute she was at our old gate!"

Brenda shrugged but Sheila's face was grey at the recollection of it.

"I asked her where she'd been," she continued, "and she said she'd met a new boy at school called Frank and taken a walk with him."

"So?" Brenda shrugged again.

"Well, when I told her it was good that she'd let you know she said she hadn't seen you since you walked to school that morning. She reminded me that you'd been on a school trip that day!"

"Did you ask me how I knew then?"

"Of course, I did but I didn't want to alarm you too much."

"What did I say?"

"You said he was a tall boy with black hair, and it must have been the day before. But when I asked Amelia about a new boy, she said that it had been his first day!"

"Wow. Did you ask me about her walking by the co-op then?"

"No. I didn't. I stopped asking lots of things that might cause you both to realise how often this stuff was going on. Why are you asking about it now?"

"Because I've got a strange feeling. Like something isn't right. Like an uneasiness of something bad going on. It feels just like when I used to sense that Amelia was in trouble."

"You think Amelia is somewhere in trouble?"

"No. Not Amelia. Frankie."

"Frankie?"

"Yes, I think I'm connecting to Frankie like I used to with Amelia! Do you think it might be hereditary?"

"I hope not!"

"Why would you say that?"

Sheila felt like she had already said too much but Brenda was no longer a child. She could make up her own mind.

"Because you have no idea as to the extent of this weird connection between you and Amelia and, if I'm totally honest, I think her disappearance had something to do with it."

"How? In what way?"

"I have no idea, but I know she used to do the same thing with Frank, and we all know that Frank was already dead when she shot out of the house to find him. She said she was only gone ten minutes and you know what? I believed her! But I also believed that she was the common denominator in it all."

"Common denominator?"

"Yes. First it was her and you, then her and Frank. He called her an open book, as I recall! Then even Brian managed to pick up on it and he's hardly a spiritual soul! He still managed to sense her plan to leave him! No good came of any of it but I always believed Amelia was the catalyst! Her and that damn clearing in the wood."

"You think there's something strange about the gap in the trees!" She laughed.

"No, I don't but I think Amelia did and that was enough to put her in the right head space to connect to something. To someone."

"I must admit that when I went there with her and gazed up like that it did feel kind of weird. Mystical and unworldly. Like gazing right through the gates to another world."

"Exactly! It created the environment she needed to make it all happen at the start then she just learned to do it anywhere, but that place was the nucleus of it all!"

"I have to say that I always got a feeling of panic when I did that with her. I was always relieved to get away again."

"Well, that should be enough of a warning so, whatever's going on with you and Frankie you need to make it stop. Promise me!"

Brenda could feel Sheila's fear as plainly as she could see it contorting her face.

"I hear you. It's just that sometimes I feel like I'm feeling what she feels and it's not good. It's always when she's with Malcolm. Like there's something bad going on whenever she's with him."

"Now listen to me. You must let Frankie live her own life. Do you hear me? No good ever came of meddling in another person's love-life."

Sheila grabbed Brenda's hands again and held them tightly until she felt submission and then she released them gently.

"I know you're right. I just want this so badly for her."

"I know you do, and I do too. Watching Frankie walk down the aisle would be the happiest day of my life, I think, but we just need to let things take their course."

Brenda tried to do just that.

She listened to Annette's reports of the nights Malcolm arrived home much later than Frankie and even of the nights he didn't go home at all, but she stopped reporting any differences to the woman who was clearly elated by the progress of this blooming romance.

By the end of the year, both Brenda and Anette were expecting something special that Christmas.

For Brenda and Sheila, Christmas always marked family bonding no matter how numerous or sparce the members. Christmas was special even if the places at the Christmas dinner table caused hearts to ache for those who used to occupy those seats.

Somehow, Sheila and Brenda still managed to make the occasion a celebration of those who remained. They were still family, and family was all that mattered.

Brenda always insisted on setting a place for Amelia even though Sheila would protest on the effect the empty chair had on Frankie.

"Setting that place gives her hope that her mother might suddenly walk back through that door, Bren. It's cruel." Sheila had snapped the first time Brenda did it after Brian's incarceration.

"It's fine." Frankie whispered from the doorway. "It's not like dad is going to sit there anyway."

From that year onwards, a place was always set for Amelia on the understanding that it was not a place they expected to be occupied but a gesture that wherever she was, she was still a part of the family.

This year, however, Brenda was hoping that the table would be too full to continue that tradition.

This year she was expecting Malcolm and his parents to be invited and secretly, she was also hoping that there might be an announcement to be made.

As she planned the event, she was budgeting for six and as she lay awake thinking of gifts and parlour games, she was imagining Malcolm on one knee with a beautiful engagement ring in his hand.

That night Brenda fell asleep with a smile on her face. A smile that was about to be replaced by a huge grin the next morning.

It was late November on the morning Brenda was rushing for work after allowing herself an extra half hour under the warmth of the covers.

She'd missed her bathroom slot, so she ran downstairs to boil the kettle and use the downstairs toilet after hearing the shower in full flow.

As she went back upstairs to pick out her clothes, she hammered on the bathroom door.

"Hurry up Frankie, I need a shower too and I'm already late."

She heard Frankie call back and rushed into her room to gather an outfit together before returning to the bathroom door with renewed urgency.

"Come on Frankie!"

"I'm coming! I'm coming!"

Frankie rushed out and Brenda rushed in with half a cup of tea and an armful of clothes.

She showered as quickly as she could, but the slamming of the door told her that she was even later than she thought. Frankie was already on her way to work!

She grabbed the towel from the hook and flung it round her, sending the small bathroom bin hurtling across the floor.

"I don't have time for this!" She muttered to the great unknown as she scurried to stuff everything back in the bin.

Then, there it was!

That little plastic stick with its huge blue message!

She stared at it for several seconds before clasping it to her chest as though it was already the child that she would love with all her heart.

Frankie was pregnant!

Twenty minutes later she was on her way to work oblivious to how late she was. The only thing that mattered today was that little stick of happiness that she would shortly be sharing with Annette.

"I've covered for you." Annette whispered as she strode in. "I said you were in the toilet."

"Thanks." Brenda beamed. "I've got something to show you."

She glanced at the two patients who were staring at the wall in the waiting area and then retrieved the item from her handbag and nudged to get Anette's attention.

"You're kidding!" Annette whispered.

"I don't think these things play jokes." She replied with a smile.

"I don't believe it!" Annette's voice was more of a squeal. "You're pregnant?"

"Of course, I'm not pregnant! I found it in the bathroom bin! Frankie's pregnant!"

Annette's face turned instantly from shock to beaming.

"We are going to be grandparents? Oh my God. We are going to be grandparents!"

"She doesn't know I've seen it so keep it to yourself for now, but I've got a feeling this Christmas is going to be a very special one.

For the rest of the day neither Annette nor Brenda could think of anything else. A huge weight had been finally lifted.

But, for Brenda, the news had only lightened the burden. The burden that time was running out still existed for herself and the race to find her sister before it was too late for her reconciliation with Brian.

Ever since that second disappearance Brenda had comforted herself with the dream that one day Amelia would return and thank her enormously for stepping in and taking care of Frankie for her. That dream had initially been based on the timescale of a year. The timescale they had all been working to and she had visualised Amelia scooping six-year-old Frankie up in her arms and crying her gratitude onto Brenda.

Even after the watershed of one year had passed, that same hope always grew on the anniversary of her disappearance. Anniversaries that came and went until Frankie was no longer a little girl who could be scooped up. She had become a disillusioned barren woman and Brenda's heart ached with regret and desperation with each disappointment. With the urgency for something to change because time was running out and soon it would all be too late. Amelia had already missed just about everything a mother cherishes but now, at least, something had been fixed. She could sigh her relief that motherhood had not passed Frankie by. It had not been too late for that.

By lunchtime both Annette and Brenda had been unable to stop themselves from planning and anticipating. Guessing the gender, suggesting names, making mental lists of everything a newborn was going to need.

"Don't you think we are getting ahead of ourselves?" Brenda frowned when Anette handed her the list she'd been making between patients.

"Yes, I do but it's such fun, isn't it?"

"Yes, it is. You missed off a bottle prepping machine by the way."

"What the hell is one of those?"

"It's a machine to replace the boiling, shaking and cooling while the baby screams." Brenda laughed.

Annette scribbled it on her list and then looked back to Brenda with a serious expression.

"You don't think she'll get rid of it do you?"

Brenda's excitement evaporated just as quickly. She hadn't given the notion any consideration.

"Of course, she won't!" She replied harshly. "Frankie loves children. She would never do such a thing. I mean, they are solid as a couple, aren't they?"

"Well, I think so but it's not like they live in each other's pockets, is it? Not like those lovers who can't bear to be apart! I mean, they tend to meet a few times a month, but they don't spend hours cooing on the phone, do they?"

Brenda could feel the weight returning. Perhaps Frankie had done the test in private because she had no intention of giving birth to this baby! No intention of parenting it with the man she has occasional dates with, but who has not captured her heart. The more Brenda thought about it, the more likely it seemed.

"I'm going to ask her tonight!" She announced with the determination of a person who couldn't bear to live with the uncertainty a second longer.

"No! Don't back her into a corner. Let me talk to Malcolm about their relationship. He'll be honest with me about how they feel and where it's going if I ask. I'll ring you after I've had the conversation then you can decide if you want to speak with Frankie."

Brenda agreed but when she arrived home that evening it felt like torture to be in Frankie's company with this huge secret hanging between them.

As ever, she turned to Sheila to unload.

"I don't think you need to worry about her aborting this baby at all." Sheila soothed. "Frankie is a compassionate woman and even if this Malcolm isn't the love of her life, I think she will keep it. In a few years she'll hit forty. This might be her last chance and if I know our Frankie, she'll grab it with both hands!"

Brenda felt just as comforted by Sheila's words as she had as a child.

"Thanks." She sighed. "I think I'll go take my mind off things by dying my grey roots while I wait for Anette to call."

"You are still my little blonde beauty you know." Sheila grinned. "You always will be. Golden hair and golden heart I used to say to your dad."

Both women instantly took a moment.

It was a moment of individual reflection. Very different perspectives of the same painful memories. The days when Sheila lived in that house with their dad. When Amelia and

Brenda shared a room and listened to them chatting happily downstairs. The days when they would go out on their bikes and race around the driveway of this very house. Fantasising about living in it together one day.

Brenda knew instantly that they were both sharing that burden again. The fear and knowledge that time was running out. That this family was still waiting for Amelia and always would be.

Brenda shut herself in the bathroom and dyed, rinsed, and towelled her hair. She then went into her room and tried to dry it with short bursts of the hair dryer, fearful of missing the ring of the phone.

That evening the phone didn't ring.

Chapter 18

Before Brenda had entered the office, she had already noticed that Annette's coat was not on the rack.

It was still twenty minutes before the surgery opened but Annette was always the first to arrive on reception.

The cleaner was just finishing off and one doctor was already in his office.

Something was wrong. She could feel it.

The reception telephone rang.

"Hello, this is Annette's husband. I'm sorry but she's not feeling well and won't be in today."

"Oh. This is Brenda. We met at my dinner party."

"Oh yes. I remember." He stuttered uncomfortably.

"So, what's wrong with Annette?" She blurted. "Shall I call in to see her at lunchtime."

"No. She's in bed. I'll call again tomorrow and let you know how she is. Please pass this on to the doctors."

She heard the receiver click.

A surge of panic surged through her. Something wasn't right. She could feel it. Something bad had happened and she needed to know what.

She muddled her way through the morning but as soon as the clock hit twelve, she was out of the door with coat in hand, hurtling across the village to Annette's house, striding up the path and hammering on the door.

As the door opened, Brenda was already calling Annette's name as she pushed by the small, slightly built man and headed for the stairs.

He didn't protest either physically or verbally. He seemed numb or broken. Whatever had happened, had hit them both.

As she reached the top step, she tried to compose herself before gently pushing open one door after another. Behind the third door was a double bed in a room still darkened by curtains. On the far side lay a mound beneath the sheets which she assumed to be Annette. The mound didn't react as she let in the light from the hallway.

"Annette?" She asked softly.

The mound remained still and quiet.

She walked over and sat down beside it before pulling back the blanket that covered Annette's head.

"Annette!"

"Leave me alone."

"Annette. What's happened? Is this something to do with Frankie? Is this about our grandchild."

"We don't have a grandchild." Annette snapped without moving.

Brenda's heart turned cold.

"What do you mean? We saw the test only yesterday!"

The silence resumed.

"Annette! What's going on? How can we not have a grandchild?"

Annette turned onto her back and peered into Brenda's anxious blue eyes. The hair she'd piled on top this morning was tumbling around her face yet still, she looked wonderful. A proper glamourous granny if ever there was one. Not like herself who would have been the ugly, fat granny. The unfairness of it all consumed her once more as Brenda recaptured an unruly blonde ringlet and re-secured it.

"Annette! Please tell me what's going on. Are you saying there is no baby?"

The woman pulled herself upright and glowered.

"Oh no. There's a baby alright. There's a grandchild for you but there's just not one for me! I should have known it. Nothing good ever happens to me!"

Brenda tried desperately to hide her relief as her brain quickly re-assessed the situation. So, Frankie was pregnant, but Malcolm was not the father. Selfishly, she allowed the news to rewarm her frozen heart. There was still a baby on the way!

She watched Annette's puffy eyes as they studied her reaction and tried quickly to mask the re-ignition of joy.

The poor woman was devastated.

She was suffering the loss of a dream just as Brenda had been only a few seconds ago.

She stroked the woman's short, tangled curls and spoke softly.

"Are you sure the baby isn't Malcolm's? How do you know?

But even before the words were spoken, Brenda knew that the answer was irrelevant to her. She was going to have a baby in her arms no matter who the father was and there was a chance that he was someone equally as suitable as Malcolm. Someone Frankie truly loved. Not someone she met up with on some sort of schedule of duty.

Already, amid Annette's misery, Brenda was imagining a whirlwind romance that had swept Frankie off her feet and conceived her a child in one fell swoop.

She tried desperately to push the excitement back down and offer some comfort to the victim of Frankie's behaviour.

"How do I know?" Annette snapped. "How do I know!"

Brenda pulled her close.

"Well, it might still be his. I mean, they have been seeing each other very regularly."

"No, they haven't." Annette sighed. "They have both been seeing someone but not each other."

"How do you know that?"

"Because I was stupid enough to arrive home yesterday with a card of congratulations for my son! How could I think that any congratulations would ever be warranted in this house?"

"What did he say?"

"Oh! Not much really. Just that he hadn't been seeing Frankie at all apart from an occasional coffee now and again."

"That was it? That's all he told you."

"Oh. There was just one more thing. I almost forgot. Silly me. He also said that he hadn't been seeing Frankie because he's gay."

"What?"

"My son is gay. Apparently. He even asked if I wanted to meet his boyfriend! The man he's been meeting while using Frankie as an alibi!"

Brenda was re-thinking the situation again.

If this hadn't been a recent whirlwind romance, then who had Frankie been seeing and why did she need to hide it?

Annette watched the questions scurry over her face and sighed again.

"And before you ask, no, I don't know what Frankie was doing on the nights my son was having sex with another man and I don't really care. I'm never going to be a grandma and I'm probably not even going to be a mother anymore. Malcom left last night, and I don't blame him after all the terrible things I called him."

At last, Brenda's selfishness was pushed aside by the look on that poor woman's face. This was no time to be second-guessing her own lot but the time to be helping her friend.

"Now listen here, Annette. I don't know of any parent who wouldn't react in the same way but that doesn't mean you've lost him. It doesn't matter who he sleeps with or who he loves. What matters is that he loves you and you love him. That's it! And now, you have a choice. You either disown him and live the rest of your life wallowing in that bed, or you show him that your love for him is stronger than anything else!"

She felt Annette stiffen slightly.

"I don't know if I can live with this."

"Of course, you can. It's just been a shock but that will wear off! Your son is out there feeling abandoned and let down even though he's a grown man. You are still his mother, and you should feel happy that he's found someone he loves. So many people don't. You might not be welcoming a grandchild into your family right now, but you have the chance to welcome a new son-in-law. A person who probably loves your son as much as you do."

She felt Annette squeeze her hand.

"I've been an idiot, haven't I? I've acted in the way I swore I never would. It was easy to swear that when it's not happening to you though."

"I know."

Annette swung her legs onto the floor and stood up.

"Will you tell them at the surgery that I'll be back in tomorrow?"

"Of course. What are you going to do this afternoon."

"I'm going to take my friend's advice." She said, more positively. "I'm going to go to his office to tell him to get himself back here and to ask him when I can meet this man that he wants to make a life with!"

The two women smiled simultaneously, hugged and then Brenda headed back for the stairs.

As she opened the front door, she waved at the little man in the living room who nodded his acknowledgement glumly, and then she made her way back to the surgery with a slightly lighter heart.

Her afternoon was just as difficult to get through as the morning had been.

Unanswered questions presented themselves constantly. Possible reasons, scenarios and catastrophes played over and over in her head.

Tonight, Annette would be re-building her relationship with her son. All secrets and lies would be laid to rest and they would be going forward with a new understanding. A new acceptance and a deeper love.

She knew that, for Annette, the worst was over, but as she packed up her bag to leave and took her coat from the hook, she knew that her ordeal still lay ahead.

She had failed to come up with a rational explanation for Frankie's covert dates. Whoever had fathered this child had led to the deceit she never believed would exist between her and daughter. She thought Frankie told her everything and the revelation that she'd been sneaking around and lying hurt like hell.

Fear and anger took turns to consume her on that walk home. The most likely reason had to be that the father was a married man. Someone happily married who had used Frankie for fun and recreation.

Annette had survived her part of this ordeal but as she opened the gate and walked down that circular drive to the front door, she knew that unlike Annette, she still had a mountain to climb.

Whatever the explanation, it wasn't going to be wonderful or joyous.

The image of a white wedding, a family christening standing beside Annette in huge hats had suddenly metamorphosed into images of shared custody, an angry vindictive wife and an unsettled, screaming child being torn from this family and thrust into another on alternative weekends.

"Where's Frankie?" She snapped as she kicked off her shoes and Sheila headed for the living room with steaming tea.

"I was going to ask you the same question." Sheila frowned.

Chapter 19

Frankie hadn't gone home after work that evening.

Her mobile phone had been vibrating throughout the morning with attempted calls from Malcolm.

At lunchtime she tried to call him back, but it went straight to voicemail.

She opened her messages.

"Meet me at our place after work. The cat is out of the bag. We need to talk."

She stayed in the classroom until five staring at the raindrops as they trickled down the window, and then went to the country pub down the road to wait for Malcolm.

"You look terrible. I got you a coffee with a shot of brandy." She soothed.

Malcom removed his jacket, shook the rainwater from it and took a mouthful without complaining that he had to drive.

He sat down opposite and simply looked at her.

Instinctively she reached for his hand to comfort him.

"What happened? Who knows what, and how?"

Malcom didn't answer.

He simply put his head in both hands and gave a huge sigh.

Frankie didn't want to appear selfish, but she was anxious to assess her own situation and that meant knowing which parents knew what.

She pulled the clasp from her nape bun and allowed her long hair to fall over her shoulders as though a softening in her appearance might somehow soften the atmosphere.

"Malcolm?"

He glanced up and tried to smile. It was always difficult not to smile when Frankie was around, and now she was looking right at him with those huge eyes and acres of hair cascading like a fairytale mermaid.

He stroked his thumb over the hand that was still holding his and sighed again.

"Well, everyone knows I'm gay for a start. I told them yesterday and then spent the night on a mate's sofa."

"They threw you out?"

"They might as well have but don't worry. Adam and I have more than enough savings to get a place of our own. He's taking the day off tomorrow to find us a place to rent for now and I'm going to work on finding a place to buy. It's probably given us the shove we needed."

Frankie could hear elements of excitement in his voice from behind the devastation of his parents' rejection of him and she felt suddenly annoyed that he'd blown up their lives without consulting her.

"Why didn't you warn me you were going to confess? I could have been prepared!"

"Ah, well that was a bit difficult." He replied a little sarcastically. "You see, I walked in last night to the euphoria of expectant grandparents! The air was electric with visions of weddings and baby-showers!"

"What!"

"It seems that I was not the only one not being warned that things were about to blow up!"

Frankie's huge eyes became even bigger as her mouth dropped open.

"It seems that you are pregnant?" Malcolm continued as he ran his fingers through his wet wiry curls.

"But how would they know that?"

"It seems that you left the test stick in the bathroom bin?"

Frankie felt the full blow of the realisation that this was all her fault.

"But I shoved it right to the bottom of the bag and covered it with wet wipes and cleansing pads! How on earth..?"

"It doesn't matter how, does it? What matters is that they all know we are not a couple. I wanted to warn you because I didn't want you being caught off guard the way I was last night."

"I know and I'm grateful." She tightened her grip on his hand. "I really am, Malcolm. Thank you."

He nodded and let his hand remain in hers.

"So, what now?"

"I really have no idea."

"Well, I don't think your mum will kick you out anyway. Seems like she's already looking for a pram from what I gathered. Between her and that Sheila, I expect the nursery will be ready by the time you get home!"

Frankie was already praying that Malcolm was right.

In the meantime, she needed to put that aside and focus on the two of them and the alliance they had forged.

"So, it seems like this is a parting of the ways?" She said softly.

He gave a little laugh.

She instantly pulled him towards her over the table and hugged his neck.

"I feel like a couple of kids who just got caught skipping school." He laughed. "I mean, we knew this day would come, didn't we? It was always going to happen."

"Yep." She concurred. "But we didn't do much preparation for it, did we?"

"Nope. None at all, really."

"So, is this it, then?"

"You mean a parting of the ways? Well, there isn't much parting to be done really, is there? Since we were never really seeing each other in the first place!"

"You know what I mean." She said irritably.

"Yes, I do. We've had each other's backs for what? Over a year now? So yes, I will miss the hurried phone calls and the frantic text messages to keep our diaries aligned. I'll miss our late-night chats and I'll miss having someone to confide in. I'll also miss this place."

"Yes, me too. It's not like we've met here that often, but it still feels like our place, doesn't it?"

"Yes, it does." He smiled. "It will always be our place."

"I suppose it still could be if we wanted?" She suggested tentatively.

"I was kind of hoping you might say that."

"So, we are going to stay in touch?"

"Well, I'd like to, if you do? I'm already thinking that I might need a suit for the christening."

She released his hand from hers, stood up and gave him a kiss on the cheek.

"I'll definitely be needing a Godfather! Or a couple of Godfathers. Men are a bit sparce in my family!"

It was an empty promise and they both knew it. They had both served a purpose in each other's lives and now it was time to go their separate ways.

He stepped around the table and pulled her close.

"I really hope this goes well for you Frankie. But if it doesn't and you need a place to stay.."

"I know." She replied solemnly. "I know exactly where to go and thank you."

He folded his arms around her so tightly that she felt he might never let her go and she didn't try to fight it. They were like two lost souls clinging together for the comfort and strength they could draw from one another, before they faced whatever was to come.

Eventually he loosened his grip and pushed her back to arm's length to see her face. Her tears mirrored his own and he looked satisfied to know it.

As he turned for the door, she grabbed her own coat and caught up.

Neither of them wanted to be the one left alone in that place. It felt too painful to contemplate being abandoned by the other, so they left hand in hand until they reached the two cars that were parked side by side just as they often had been.

He walked her over to hers and held both her hands in his as he faced her.

"Everything is going to be fine. This is how you planned it, remember. This is the final hurdle and you're going to fly over it!"

She nodded numbly. Words were no longer an option in her choked throat.

She plonked herself behind the wheel and watched him drive away as he wound down the window.

"Call me." He ordered.

"I will. I promise."

The feeling of abandonment she'd tried to avoid, descended anyway, and the promise had already been broken into a thousand pieces.

She was alone now, and this was her own mess to sort out.

She drove slowly to give herself thinking time but the only thoughts that were hurtling through her brain were doubts.

Until that moment she hadn't realised just how much Malcolm's involvement in this had been a comfort to her. Regardless of the circumstances, they had been in this together and somehow that had established them as a partnership, a couple.

Now, as she drove home alone, she felt more abandoned than she had for many years.

Suddenly the pain of those early months when her mummy went missing became almost touchable again. The nights she'd cried in Brenda's arms and asked repeatedly where her mummy had gone. The bewilderment of kissing her grandad goodbye as he left for Scotland when she was five years old. The same pain she'd felt when her daddy had been hauled off by the police when she was ten and the subsequent removal of Barry from her life who she'd loved dearly.

The only constants in her life were Sheila and the woman she had renamed as her mum. The ever-loving Brenda.

As she pulled up on that driveway, she prayed to God that the two women who had stood by her through every storm would not abandon her now.

Chapter 20

As the front door clicked open and she gently pushed against it she could already sense the atmosphere inside.

Through that small gap she was sure she could feel the denseness of the air inside seeping through. Air charged with a current of anticipation and heavy with the dread of revelation.

She hung up her coat and listened.

In the living room the television was playing quietly. A subtle invitation to enter the witness box, the confession box!

She recalled Malcolm's words.

"This is the last hurdle and you're going to fly over it."

She took a deep breath and tried to muster those wings before walking confidently into the living room.

Sheila quickly flicked the remote and silenced the television, but her mum didn't react at all.

Frankie could feel the emotion in the air between them and it wasn't anger or bitterness. It was something far worse. The atmosphere was thick and heavy with nothing other than pain. The woman who had loved and supported her, taken over the role of mothering her and sacrificed her own dreams for her, was hurting and Frankie was absorbing it as tangibly as dry sand greets an incoming wave.

The pain Brenda had been bearing all afternoon was now being shared. Silently and gradually, it was seeping from one to the other.

Frankie's rehearsed opening speech was swept away by the force of it and she simply stood in the doorway and allowed the tears to flow.

Brenda looked up for a second and sighed.

She then did exactly as Frankie had hoped. She stood up and walked over with arms outstretched.

There was no room for indignation here. No room for selfish pride or reprisal of being tricked. As always, there was never any room for anything else with Brenda. All the room was taken up with the enormity of a mother's love.

As she approached with those arms outstretched Frankie broke down completely. Before Brenda could embrace her, she was already sobbing.

Sobbing for the betrayal, for the months and months of lies and for the pain she knew she had caused but she was also crying from the guilt that, no matter how much devotion her mum gave to her, there was always that longing deep inside for her mummy. The woman who's touch she could still remember and who would never be completely replaced no matter how hard she tried to return the love she was seeing right now.

"I suppose this is the time when you ask me who the father is?" She said quietly.

"I guess it is." Brenda replied with equal serenity.

Sheila remained silent.

"Well, the truth is that I don't know."

"How can you not know, Frankie? You've been seeing this man for a year!"

"No, I haven't."

"I don't understand. All these dates that you tried to disguise as dates with Malcolm. They must have been with someone?"

"They weren't dates, mum. They were just random nights out. Here and there, clubs and bars, towns, and villages away from here. Any place I wouldn't be recognised."

"I really don't know what you're telling me, Frankie!" Brenda was starting to become frustrated.

"I think what she's saying love," Sheila interrupted, "is that she's been out trying to get herself pregnant with any man who could do the job but without ties, am I right Frankie?"

Frankie nodded as her face started to crumple again.

"What!" Brenda snapped. "Why? Why would you want to do such a thing?"

Frankie looked to Sheila who nodded approvingly. Sheila had already joined the dots, but Brenda needed to hear it from her daughter.

"Oh mum. I wanted a child so badly. I really did and my clock was ticking without a man in sight, so I decided to just do it. To get a child of my own that no-one could take away."

"Why would anyone take it away?" Brenda frowned.

"I didn't want a child who would be pulled back and forth between parents. Spending Saturdays in MacDonalds with a father who hardly knew it, or missing a friend's birthday party because he couldn't be bothered to take it on his day. And I didn't want any feisty grandparents trying to take it away like the Gilbert's did with me. I didn't want it to go through any of that! I wanted to be able to have this baby all the time. Just mine."

Until that moment, Brenda had never linked all the losses and abandonments Frankie had suffered. She wanted her child to herself because she didn't trust anyone else to stay.

"I think this is the time you call me a slut and an irresponsible idiot." Frankie sighed.

Brenda just pulled Frankie close and hugged her with all her might.

"I would never call you any of those things and don't you worry. This baby is going to have the happiest, safest life with us. With all of us, you hear?"

She turned Frankie's face up to meet hers and repeated the question.

"You hear me."

"I hear you."

Brenda then took each of Frankie's hands in hers.

"I think you are blooming already, young lady!" She smiled.

Frankie smiled back but with a little less contentment.

She was grateful and she was relieved. Happy and excited for what lay ahead but there was still something missing. As she held her mum's hands in hers, she could feel the love and affection, but she knew that if those hands had been those of her mummy's she would have felt boundless reassurance through those fingers. A feeling she would never feel again from Amelia but a feeling she hoped to feel again very soon when she held her own child in her arms.

For the months that followed, Brenda became busy in collecting things for the baby, redecorating a nursery and trying desperately not to rub Annette's nose in her good fortune.

She did, however, play a huge part in repairing the relationship between Malcolm and his parents and although he bought a place with Adam, they were slowly building a family of their own.

Frankie announced that she wanted to continue working after her maternity leave so the finances were duly re-assessed.

The house was already paid in full, so it seemed sensible for Frankie to return to work and for Brenda to reduce her hours and take the evening shifts no-one else wanted. With both wages and Sheila's pension they would be fine. The odd hours of overlap here and there would be covered by Sheila who was still quite capable of caring for a baby for an hour or so.

"You actually like this idea of the three of us raising a baby, don't you?" Sheila asked Brenda one day while they were alone.

"I guess I do. What's wrong with that?"

"You really don't know, Brenda?"

"No, I don't. Are you going to spoil this for me?"

Brenda knew that Sheila would never try to spoil anything, but it didn't prevent her from accusing the woman of doing just that if she was about to offer some unwelcome words of wisdom.

Brenda already knew that the plan was flawed but she was choosing to ignore the red flags that Sheila was about to waft in her face.

"I'm not trying to spoil any of this, love. You know that. It's a wonderful blessing to be able to nurture a child and the three of us will do a marvellous job of it."

"But?"

Sheila laughed.

"But you already know what the fly in the ointment is."

"Do I?"

"Yes, you do. You know that this determination to exclude anyone else will prevent Frankie from ever experiencing love."

"She will have enough love right here. The love of a family and of her child."

"You know what I'm talking about, Bren. The love between lovers! She's had nothing other than a frenzy of one-night stands with drunken men or reckless boys. If she stays on this path, she's going to miss out on one of life's most wonderful experiences."

"But she'll be spared the agony of that same experience. Look at us two. It didn't get us very far, did it?"

Sheila let the silence speak for itself.

Neither of them would have swapped those years of pleasure and pain for a life of celibacy, regardless of the penalties they paid for it.

"I think it's the wrong time for her to be looking for a man right now though, don't you?" Brenda said, defensively.

"Yes, it is but I think we should maybe help her to put her own demons aside and start to open up to the idea of letting someone into her life at some point?"

"Ok. I've heard you and, as usual, you're right but for now can we just enjoy the moment?"

"Of course." Sheila smiled. "Of course, we can."

Brenda extended her hand, and the two women shook on it. It was an understanding between them to make the most of the joy that lay ahead but not to lose sight of the long-term goal to make sure Frankie didn't miss out on the other precious joy life has to offer. The joy of falling insanely in love.

It was with the satisfaction of making that pact that they were then able to totally indulge themselves in the delights and extravagance of preparing for the new addition to their unconventional family.

Part of that preparation presented her with the perfect excuse to contact Brian. She wrangled with the decision for several weeks before sharing her dilemma with Sheila.

"I'm sure he would want to know. He was her father for ten years after all but are you sure you can handle it? Wouldn't it be better to just send him an email or something?"

Brenda smiled.

"I can handle it."

"Well, I wouldn't tell Frankie if I were you. On your own head be it."

As she turned away to load the dishwasher, the smile remained.

Sheila had just given her the green light and handling a meet-up with Brian was something she'd been longing for throughout the lonely years that had passed since that farewell kiss in the carpark.

Suddenly she could think of nothing else.

Chapter 21

Brian's feet were the only bit of him she could see as she tottered into the dimly lit garage in high heels, but those huge feet were unmistakeable as they protruded from a jacked-up car.

"How many times have I told you to use the pit?" She chastised. "You'll get yourself killed!"

The trolly emerged slowly from beneath the car. So slowly that she already knew he was holding his breath in anticipation. Bit by bit his overalls emerged, and she could feel every nerve in her body start to tingle. He was savouring every second of this moment of reunion.

She waited for the moment when his huge smile would appear.

The trolly continued to roll but as his face finally came into view his expression caused her own smile to fade. This was no longer a man capable of mustering a cheery 'hello' but a man incapable of hiding his heartache.

He pulled himself to his feet and then looked down on her with his doleful eyes fixed rigidly on hers. She had never seen him like this before. He seemed totally lost. Lost and numb.

"I came to tell you something." She said apologetically.

"Is Amelia back?"

"No. No, it's not that."

He answered with an enormous sigh of disappointment.

"You're still hoping for that to happen?"

"Of course, I am. It's the only way now that Frankie will ever be sure I didn't hurt her mummy."

Brenda noticed how, just like Frankie, he still referred to Amelia as her mummy. Like time had stood still for both of them. Amelia would never hold the name 'mum' or 'mother' because her memory was frozen in time.

Brian quickly recovered from disappointment back to the fear of what was so important to bring Brenda here.

"Are you getting married?"

He was already looking her up and down accusingly as though she might have dressed up to deliver the blow.

"No! Of course not!"

He frowned but didn't speak, causing her to fill the awkward silence.

"Of course, I'm not getting married! I've told you a thousand times that there's only one man I'd ever marry and he's this oily mess standing right in front of me!"

She watched the pain melt from his face and the tears of relief take its place.

"I'm sorry, I just thought.."

She reached for his huge knobbly, greasy hand and nodded her acceptance of his apology.

"I came to let you know that Frankie is having a baby."

"A baby? Did I miss the wedding?"

"No. You didn't. It's a long story."

"And I have a long lunchbreak." He smiled.

She followed him into the small office which was now surprisingly smart with its computer screens, printer and coffee maker.

Instantly she noticed the second screen at an empty desk.

"You have a new apprentice?"

He rolled his eyes and then shook his head.

"I intended to have an apprentice. Whole new start-up after my dad let it all go to pot, but it seems," he took a breath, "it seems that no-one is comfortable with having a murderer as their son's boss!"

"Or daughters." She corrected.

"Oh yes, I'd forgotten you were a pioneer for sexual equality!"

The mood had been lightened for a moment, but Brian quickly returned to the facts.

"I do have an assistant but he's a bit long in the tooth I'm afraid. That computer over there has barely been touched. He writes everything on bits of paper and leaves them on my desk. Sometimes he covers it with a tablecloth and sticks a vase on it! He's a frustrating pain in the arse."

Brenda was already imagining herself at that desk. Of being the friendly, helpful face to welcome customers and to see Brian every day as she helped him to erase the stigma of his crime.

"And no. You can't help me with it."

"What makes you think I was going to suggest it?"

"You were staring at that screen as though it was calling to you to sit in front of it!" He laughed.

"Am I that obvious?"

He walked over to the coffee machine and switched it on without replying.

"White, no sugar?"

She nodded and watched his dirty hands stick a cup under the jet. The years had passed but those hands were still the same hands that used to dirty her washing up water when he came up from behind and plunged them into the bowl. She remembered how she would flick water over her shoulder at him in playful retaliation, and how he would rub bubbles into her face as his long arms immobilised her. Those were the good days that created the good years she still longed for so desperately, but it all seemed too late now.

As he removed the steaming China cup and replaced it with his greasy, cracked mug she was reminded of the way he always made her feel like a lady.

Perhaps it wasn't too late?

The first question he'd asked was if Amelia had returned and subconsciously, he had reinforced what she already knew. Brian hadn't been responsible for Amelia's disappearance and if she could convince Frankie of it then maybe there was still a chance for them?

As he prized the lid off a dirty tin and tipped out a few broken biscuits onto a plate she was already feeling excited at the prospect of it.

She imagined herself behind that desk with the determination to get this business back on its feet.

"Why are you smiling?" Brian asked suddenly.

"Was I? I think it's just so lovely to see you again." She lied.

He broke a chunk of biscuit into his mouth with those protruding teeth and grinned.

She returned the grin. He was still the same ugly, ungainly clown she remembered but he still had her heart in the palm of those dirty hands. This was the man who used to whisper to her in the dark in those moments when all physicality became invisible, and she could feel the beauty of what lay inside. Those huge dirty hands would feel so gentle against her skin as they caressed her body and caused her to shudder with anticipation. His mouth would find hers and never once had she noticed those huge teeth in his skilful kisses. His kisses had been as sensual and delicate of any she had ever felt before and as she watched him struggle to keep the chunks of crushed biscuit behind them, the whole thing suddenly felt like a miracle.

She laughed out loud.

"What's up?"

"What's up is that you are still the funniest, most attractive man in my orbit."

He gave her a playful shove to disguise the depth of his own longing for the woman who had never been out of his thoughts for a single day since he kissed her and his ten-year-old daughter goodbye on that morning so many years ago.

"I will always love you, Brian. I hope you know that?"

"Right back at ya!" He replied with a jovial tone that was so far from the tone he hid in his heart.

He pulled out a chair for her and sat opposite as though drawing an invisible line under their emotional exchanges.

"So, are you going to explain why our daughter is about to become a single mum, or what?"

For the next half hour, over a second cup of coffee, Brenda told Brian everything including her own opinion on why Frankie didn't want to share her child with anyone else.

"We did this to her." He said firmly after she'd finished the whole story.

Brenda looked instantly offended.

"We did?"

"Not you and me." He corrected. "You did nothing wrong, Bren. When I said we did this to her I was referring to myself and Amelia. We are the ones who caused this. We allowed her to believe that I was her father. We lied to her and then Amelia broke up our happy family with her damned infatuations for the boy she'd screwed only once, and in the back of an old car just a few yards from where we are right now. She ruined everything for Frankie and then I made it all even worse with my attempt to stop it all."

"Your attempt to stop it?"

"Ok.ok. So, I knocked the guy over the head. In hindsight it was probably a bit extreme."

"You think?"

He frowned at her as she slurped the remains of her drink.

Instantly, she spurted the contents of her mouth onto his legs in a burst of spontaneous laughter. His own face contorted as he tried to contain the outburst that would rival hers.

They laughed for the longest time without speaking a single word as twenty-nine years of heartache were released in those gut-wrenching spates of laughter.

Only when exhaustion calmed their aching bodies did Brenda add the one thing she wanted to say.

"All three of us carry some blame. Not just you and Mealy. I was the one who lit the blue touch paper when I handed in Amelia's case. It was me, not you or Mealy who ruined everything."

Brian pursed his lips and gave a little nod of agreement.

"I must say, I was a little disappointed that morning if I'm honest."

Brenda burst out laughing again and Brian giggled like a child.

Eventually Brenda stood up to leave and Brian hugged her close before releasing her with a gentle smile.

As she walked away, he called after her.

"Let me know how things go. About the baby!"

Brenda raised her arm in acknowledgement and got back into her car.

She drove home with a new numbness in her heart.

Brian Gilbert was, without doubt, the only man who would ever hold a place in her heart and the only man she ever wanted to hold that place.

Brenda's love life was over.

Chapter 22

A week later, as Frankie threw up for the third time that morning, Brenda marvelled at how completely the anticipation of a new life could eradicate all other feelings.

In that summer of 2014, every moment seemed to be absorbed in that anticipation as Frankie wobbled around, counting down the days amid the frantic nest-building of her two mother hens.

She opened the door to a delivery driver almost every day as one after another, essential clutter arrived for the baby. Chairs of every description stood proudly blocking doorways and corridors. Pushchair, highchair, rocking chair, bouncy chair, musical chair, not to mention the prams!

"You can't take that thing in a car!" Brenda had laughed when a driver arrived with a huge, elegant Silver Cross spring-loaded baby carriage from Sheila that looked like it had travelled through time from the fifties.

"It's beautiful though." Frankie had added as she rocked it gently in the hallway.

"Exactly!" Sheila said smugly. "This is a pram for walking round the village. It can rock a baby to sleep without you even having to touch it."

Frankie and Sheila exchanged a satisfied smile while Brenda rolled her eyes and pushed it further into the house to take its place in the traffic jam of equipment.

"I'll buy the practical pram then, shall I?" Brenda asked and disappeared into the kitchen without waiting for a reply.

She flicked on the kettle and booted up her laptop to search for a pram more suited to modern life.

During those months of chaotic preparation Brenda had no time to yearn for anything else, but occasionally she would take her laptop to bed and send Brian an email about Frankie's journey to motherhood.

The exchanges were warm and polite but neither of them ventured to cross the line to hopeless dreams of the life that could never be.

Olivia Amelia Gilbert was born on 1st September 2014 in Rochdale maternity ward in the presence of a midwife and the two mother hens who cooed, cackled, and cried as they passed the infant back and forth while Frankie lay exhausted.

Eventually the midwife managed to pry the baby from the duo and Frankie finally held her baby and allowed her feelings for her tiny daughter to flow between them.

This was it! This was the feeling she remembered from the touch of her own mummy. Of Amelia. There was no mistaking it and for that, she held her baby for the longest time. To drink it in and to allow the nostalgia to scorch her heart.

An hour later Brenda and Sheila took turns to kiss the baby and Frankie goodbye as they collected their belongings to allow her to rest.

The first thing Brenda did when she got home was to take her phone upstairs to email Brian on their secret account. The passing of time had at least delivered the freedom of communication and although the contact was infrequent, there were times when it felt like a lifeline. Knowing that she could contact him day or night without the risk of a reply dropping on the mat for all to see.

She got into bed and left her phone on the nightstand to await the familiar ping that would announce his reply within seconds of sending.

The return was a huge smiley face which was instantly mirrored on her own face.

Brian had always been a man of few words even though he brimmed with emotion, and she knew that the small, lonely face on his email contained a thousand words.

Brian had always been a man who used acts not words to convey his feelings. Gifts, surprises, effort, and deeds were his arsenal when it came to communicating his feelings.

She held the phone close for a moment and wondered if that had been the cause of their misery. If Brian had been unable to express his feelings to Amelia when he realised Frank was back on the scene? Unable to talk to her, to communicate his desperation and fear, and the result had been the swinging of that wrench. He had solved the issue with an act!

Brenda flinched as she imagined the crack on Franks skull and pulled the bedclothes over her head to hide from the horror of that image caused by the perpetrator she still loved.

She remained beneath the sheets as she muttered her nightly prayer, but tonight the prayer started with gratitude for the safe arrival of baby Olivia. Her mutterings then covered the usual plea for protection of those she loved. Those who still remained. For the good health of Brian, of Sheila and of Barry. Then for the happiness and peace of those who had passed. Of her mother and father and finally her prayer ended with the statutory, obdurate, unyielding plea for the safe return of Amelia.

Many times, over the years she had considered moving Amelia's name into the previous group, but it seemed like tempting fate or like somehow giving God permission to take her, so Amelia remained in the group of the unknown. The missing not the lost because Brenda wasn't ready to let her go. Not yet.

She placed the phone back on the nightstand and went to sleep with the same sinking feeling she'd had for the last three decades. The knowledge that time was running out. That Amelia had missed just about everything! That it was almost certain now that she would never get the chance to tell her anything at all and she would never know of the sacrifices she'd made to bring up Frankie for her.

By morning, the dread and pain had been dissolved by sleep and her mind was racing in anticipation of the big homecoming of mother and child.

"Are you going to let Barry know?" Brenda asked as she ripped open the bundles of disposable nappies and arranged them in Olivia's nursery draw.

"You might as well keep those downstairs!" Sheila exclaimed. "We'll be using more than a dozen a day!"

Brenda retrieved a large handful and tucked them under her arm.

"Did you hear what I said?"

"Yes, I heard you."

"So?"

"I doubt he'd be interested. It's not like he's related or anything and he's probably moved on by now."

Brenda watched her face flush.

She had never felt able to interrogate Sheila because the woman still held the mother status, but she knew that her feelings for Barry were far from over.

"If you say so."

"What does that mean?"

"I was talking about the nappies." Brenda grinned.

She knew for a fact that Barry was still single and was certain that Sheila knew it too. There was still some kind of game going on between them but neither of them seemed capable of having the conversation.

Brenda would sometimes park at the end of the road merely to check the status of the gnome garden which changed frequently. What had started as a game of re-arranging them seemed to have evolved into adding or removing characters, but she knew better than to accuse Sheila of such childish behaviour.

She hadn't even mentioned finding a receipt for a rather expensive gnome that inter-actively called abuse to passers-by. However, the appearance of a gnome couple, in a romantic embrace had, almost prompted her to demand that Sheila just knocks on the door and gets it over with.

The only thing holding Brenda back was the selfish fear of losing Sheila again. Having her around the house was a comfort she wasn't sure she could live without.

But today was no time for reflection because today they had a new baby to bring home.

Sheila prepared a special tea while Brenda wrestled with the Isofix base to enable the baby seat to be slotted in.

Finally, sweating and frustrated, Brenda was on her way to collect Frankie and the baby.

Like all new mothers, Frankie was an emotional wreck.

"Why are you crying?" Brenda smiled as she watched Frankie cradling Olivia in the hospital wheelchair.

"I really don't know, mum." Frankie replied. "I just feel so tired and bruised and fat and ugly and…"

"Totally overwhelmed?"

Frankie nodded.

"You'll feel much better after a warm bath, a change of clothes and a hairstyle." Brenda smiled.

"And my breasts are leaking everywhere!"

Brenda put her arms around her little family in that chair and another pledge was made. Nothing else mattered other than the strength of those arms to protect what lie inside them.

That evening Brenda slept on the floor beside Frankie to help with the night feeds and nappy changing, and that mattress remained there for several weeks.

Frankie tried hard to be a self-sufficient mother to her new baby, but it seemed that she was never really, up to it in that first couple of months. Frankie was constantly unwell.

"This sometimes happens." The midwife assured.

"But she seems to catch one thing after another!" Brenda protested. "First a cold, then a sickness bug, then a sore throat!"

The midwife could see the worry on Brenda's face. This was a woman who had lost one person after another, and she seemed to be anticipating the worst.

"I promise you that this is absolutely normal." She comforted. "Having a baby really does compromise the immune system. More so in one mother than another but it will pass. You have my word on it."

Brenda took a deep sigh and tried to bury her fear.

That day seemed to have been the turning point and as Brenda started to relax, Frankie started to feel more positive despite her frequent illnesses, and Olivia learned to smile.

Finally, Brenda allowed herself to believe that these were the good days again as she walked proudly round that driveway with her granddaughter in that beautiful pram.

That afternoon Sheila took a taxi carrying a large parcel that had arrived at the house that morning.

The taxi pulled up outside Barry's house and she carefully unwrapped the gnome of a grandma in a wicker chair cradling a baby in pink.

"Would you be kind enough to help me get out?"

The driver smiled and offered his elbow for support before sitting back in the driving seat to stare at his phone.

Sheila smiled as she placed her announcement of the birth carefully beside the embracing lovers. There was no need to tell Barry of Olivia's arrival. He would know and he would smile at her childish playfulness.

She glanced at the window in the hope of being caught red-handed, but the house no longer had curtains. She wobbled over to the window and cupped her hand over her eyes to peer inside and her heart sank.

The house was deserted. Empty and deserted.

Her sinking heart suddenly started to pound violently as she rushed to bang on the door of the attached neighbour with one thought racing through her brain. She was too late. Her stubborn behaviour had cost her the reunion and forgiveness she always intended to give.

A middle-aged woman opened the door and frowned.

"Is he dead?"

"Who?"

"Barry from next door. Is he dead?"

"And who are you?"

"I'm his partner, I mean, I'm his friend. Is he dead?"

"No." The woman snapped irritably. "He did his hip in, messing about with those hideous gnomes I expect. They took him into a nursing home a month ago, so I guess he's staying there."

Sheila felt the relief and injustice of it simultaneously.

"He would never give up his independence! He's years younger than me!"

The woman looked her up and down with amusement.

"Ok, I know that's not saying much but he would never go into a home. Not Barry."

The woman immediately huffed.

"That's the council for you! Too keen to get their hands on everything you've worked for! They'll be selling this place and using the money to pay for his incarceration."

"Do you know where they took him?"

"Yes, I have a key, so I forward all his mail onto Oakland Care Home on Bury Road."

"I know where that it. Thanks."

Sheila was already striding back down the path with no sign of her previous wobble.

"Take me to Oakland Care Home." She instructed as she plonked herself back on the seat without assistance before flicking the driver on the head with her fingers.

"Hey! Did you hear me? You can play on your phone later!"

She rehearsed her speech over and over on the journey but the moment she walked into the dayroom and saw Barry's face, every word of it disappeared.

"Barry! What are you doing in this dump. Get your things. We're leaving!"

Barry stared at her for a second, and grinned.

He didn't need an explanation because this was his Sheila and he knew her inside out. She'd wrapped up her forgiveness, regret, and love in one short sentence and he wasn't going to argue with it.

"You can't just move him out!" A carer protested. "I'll go and get my manager. Wait a minute."

"I'm not waiting any minutes for anyone!" Sheila hissed. "Is this a prison?"

"No. of course not, but…"

"But nothing. He's coming with me, and I'll send for his belongings later. Come on Barry."

Barry hobbled beside her as she hauled him to his room and grabbed a few of his belongings. Ten minutes later they were back in the taxi and on their way to Cherry Blossom house.

Brenda opened the door to them and simply beamed from ear to ear without asking a single question.

Barry was back and that was enough for now because she was already imagining him sitting at the family table again this Christmas. The days were already getting shorter and colder and this year they would be shopping for toys again. The idea warmed her to the core as she turned back into the living room and pumped-up cushions to welcome the man she had missed enormously. She then nipped out to buy a bottle of wine to celebrate, and as she turned back into that driveway, emotion welled once again as she visualised herself and Amelia straddling their bikes as they stared up at that house with a thousand dreams in their heads. Picking out their bedrooms from the windows they could see and excitedly describing the wonderful wedding of their dad and Sheila in that enormous garden. Dreams of a life that was not to be.

Despite the homecoming of Barry and Olivia, her heart still ached for the sister who had once been her world. For the days they would lay in bed and practise sending their thought waves back and forth. She remembered sometimes sensing Amelia's worries or pain even when they were miles apart. She stood on the driveway and looked up to the sky. If Amelia was still on this planet, she would surely sense it. She closed her eyes and allowed the cold breeze to empty her mind to enable her to connect to her Mealy. But her mind flowed freely in all directions. No sensation of thickening as she used to collide with her sister's thoughts. No sudden emotions or images. Nothing.

She opened her eyes and continued down the drive with a heavy heart. The dream they had shared was as dead as her sister.

But as she opened the door to the scent of family life and the chattering of familiar voices, she realised that the dream hadn't been lost at all but changed a little. She heard Barry and Sheila laughing and her heart was lifted a little.

This was a feeling she remembered.

The feeling of contentment from her childhood and she soaked it in greedily as she stood in the hallway and closed her eyes again to listen to the sound of it. The hum of family life. Laughter and love were bursting from that room amidst the sounds of a baby's gurgling and sobs of reunited joy, and this was everything she needed.

It was enough. More than enough. She had finally let go of the past. Of her own mother and father, of Brian and finally, of Amelia.

Chapter 23

Christmas time had the habit of being the milestone in this family and the Christmas of 2014 was no exception.

To Brenda, despite the momentous reunion, it would be remembered as a pleasant and contented affair but nothing more than that.

The three women worked hard to create the ultimate family Christmas, but Brenda couldn't eradicate the feeling of disappointment as the day progressed. At only three months old, Olivia was oblivious to the occasion but stubbornly they insisted on hanging a stocking, opening gifts she barely reacted to, and dressing her in an uncomfortable elf outfit which was removed only an hour later to stop her from screaming.

As Olivia slept, they sat at the table, pulled crackers and clinked glasses in a rather flat atmosphere of unified disappointment.

Brenda felt the need to say something as they cleared the table.

"I can't wait for next year when Olivia will really enjoy a Christmas!"

Frankie's heart felt immediately lightened.

"Yes. She'll be toddling around by then and we won't get a minute of peace! We should relish these moments of tranquillity because this may be the last tranquil Christmas for many years!"

Sheila winked at Brenda.

The elephant in the room had been tackled. Their expectations had been realigned and consequently their disappointment had been tempered.

They finished washing up and poured more wine before going into the lounge to watch the Queen's speech.

Within seconds Brenda's heart was aching again. Her own elephant was of a different form because the feeling was still one of a special breed of homesickness. Not for the old house but for the loved ones she could never have. Time and again, she reminded herself that this was enough but the ghosts of Christmas past seemed hell bent on haunting her again.

She looked around that lounge of so many empty seats and imagined where her dad would have sat, where Brian would sit and where Amelia would lie on the floor as she always did.

It didn't make any sense, even to her, because the return of her father would destroy the contentment of Sheila and Barry and the return of Brian and Amelia would probably reunite them as man and wife leaving her alone and miserable.

She reprimanded herself once again and reminded herself that the family she wanted was still right here. This was the only dynamic that would work now. Something she would remind herself of every day as she waited for the homesickness to pass and her longing to hold her sister and Brian in her arms again, to fade away.

But during that spring of 2015 she managed only to let go of her longing for Amelia. Her heartache for Brian refused to budge. She needed to find a way to bring him back into the fold and into her bed.

Sheila and Barry remained at Cherry Blossom but refused to give up the house that had been their love nest for so many years. They would spend many hours tending the gnome garden and cooking daytime meals there together. To them, it felt like recapturing their past but to Brenda it felt like some sort of ungrateful betrayal.

"I don't know why it bothers you so much." Frankie laughed. "They are just giving themselves a bit of space together!"

"They are like two infants playing house!" Brenda retorted. "Not capable of living independently so they go and play over there and then come home at bedtime!"

Frankie merely cocked her head and raised her eyebrows.

"It makes them happy. Why do you resent it so much?"

"I don't. I just think it's a bit pathetic."

Frankie repeated the gesture as Brenda walked away with her armful of washed baby clothes.

As she hung them over the clothes horse, she tried to contain her feelings. Frankie was right. It made them happy and that seemed to be the problem. How could she resent them a bit of happiness? So what? if they were using this house for stability and their own to play in! She slapped the Babygros haphazardly over the wires and reprimanded herself for her selfishness, for her jealousy and envy. Sheila had got her man back and she was making the most of it!

She returned to the kitchen, where Frankie was putting another load into the washer and sighed deeply.

"I was being selfish." She announced. "Sheila has done more than enough for us and if she wants to use this place as a hotel and keep Barry's for date days then she's more than welcome."

"I should think so!" Frankie smiled. "No-one should get in the way of true love."

Leigh Oakley

Brenda tried to ignore the irony as she returned the smile. Words spoken innocently by the one person who was standing directly in the path of her reunion with her beloved Brian!

But life continued and Frankie returned to work after the summer holidays leaving the curly haired little girl with the women she trusted most in this world.

Olivia's hair had grown into a mass of tight brown curls causing Frankie to wade through her memories as she tried to recall the images of the men that she'd slept with in the month she became pregnant. She tried to muddle her way through the images of blurred faces and clumsy groping to spot a head of curls like Olivia's, but the images were as vague and unremarkable as all the others that had gone before. She reminded herself that this was a good thing.

At Olivia's first Birthday party a neighbour smiled and said she suited her surname perfectly because she looked like Gilbert O'Sullivan. Consequently, she was affectionately nicknamed Gilly by everyone except Brenda who insisted on using her given name.

The brown curly hair and nickname did however reach the ears of two people in their own village and one Sunday morning Frankie opened the door to a frail old couple who arrived by taxi.

"Please don't close the door on us." The old woman begged.

Frankie studied her face and then that of the old man.

"Grandma?"

Jean smiled. "I guess I've aged a tad?"

Frankie froze for a moment as the old couple remained on the doorstep.

"What do you want?" She asked firmly.

"Just a few minutes of your time, that's all. We are not here to cause any trouble. We just want a few minutes."

Frankie fidgeted uneasily before standing aside and allowing them to shuffle into the impressive hallway.

"This is quite a place you've got here." Charlie mumbled as he continued to twist his cap over and over in his hands.

"Thank you." Frankie replied politely but coldly.

"I know what we did was wrong. Very wrong." Jean continued. "We were just terrified of losing you after what our son did. You'd been our granddaughter for ten years love, and it was so hard to lose everything like that. We were desperate and we were selfish. We just want to ask you something, but it won't change why we are here."

She pulled a well-worn photograph out of her pocket and handed it to Frankie. The baby in the pram had a mop of brown curls just like Olivia.

"Is this Brian?"

Jean nodded. "His hair was like this for over a year before it started to change into the sandy, wiry mess you'll remember."

"I guess you've seen Gilly in the pram somewhere and are wondering if my dad, I mean your Brian, was lying about not being my real father?"

Jean shrugged and Frankie tossed back her own black mane before continuing.

"No. He wasn't lying and if you want a strand of my hair or something then here, take it!"

She pulled out a long strand and thrust it at the old woman causing Charlie to put his hand out to steady her.

"Jean doesn't want anything from you Frankie, and neither do I. We have come here to try to make amends. We did a terrible thing when Brian was sentenced, and we paid for it. We paid dearly for it because we lost you."

Frankie felt their pain instantly. The outcome had been equally painful for her too. She'd already lost both her parents back then and having Jean and Charlie to cling to would have been an enormous comfort.

"I know." She said gently. "I lost you too."

Jean instinctively held out her bony arms and Frankie allowed herself to slide into them.

In an instant, the touch of her grandma invoked a sob from somewhere deep inside her soul.

"Oh, Frankie love. You have always been our Granddaughter, no matter what the science says."

She felt her grandma's hand cradle the back of her head just as it had when she was a child and the awful pain of those lost years wrenched at her stomach.

"Come in and sit down." Sheila's voice came from behind.

Frankie pulled away and tried to dry her eyes with the back of her hand.

"Yes. Come in. I'd like you to meet your Great Granddaughter."

Frankie watched them shuffle unsteadily into the living room and fall heavily onto the couch in turn.

"Time is running out for us Frankie. You can see that, and I just want to try to make some sort of amends for the terrible things my family has inflicted on yours."

"There's no need." Frankie whispered. "It's all water under the bridge now but I can't forgive dad. Not for killing my mum."

Charlie leaned forward with his cap still twirling between his white-knuckled hands.

"We're not here to ask you to forgive our son, Frankie. We have chosen to believe him to be innocent of hurting your mum, but you must trust your own instincts on it, and from your point of view it is bad enough that he killed your father."

Frankie took a few moments before replying.

"Awful as it sounds," she said meekly, "I think I could forgive him that because Frank was about to steal away everything we had. I loved your son. He was the most wonderful father and if anyone tried to break us up, I think I would have been just as desperate. I could never forgive him if he hurt my mummy though. Never."

Jean nodded sympathetically.

"So, why are you here?" Brenda interrupted as she entered the room.

"We wanted to let you know that we are leaving our half of the garage and our house to you, Frankie."

"But what about Brian?"

"He already has his half of the business, for what it's worth, and we gave him the rest of our savings for a deposit on a house of his own. He'll be fine."

"But we aren't even related!" Frankie scowled.

"Blood may be thicker than water, but love is thicker than blood." She smiled. "We have always loved you Frankie, I thought you knew that."

Frankie shook her head.

"I wish I had."

"Well, you know it now."

For the next hour, they chatted about the years that had passed, and Frankie realised that they had been such wasted years even though no-one said it out loud.

They played with Olivia, and no-one objected when they called her Gilly.

Eventually, after they fumbled for the taxi number, Brenda offered to drive them home and told them they would be welcome any time but that their son must stay away.

She helped them to the door of their smart bungalow and as they closed it, she couldn't help wondering if Brian was inside. Just a few feet away from the embrace she was aching for.

As she drove, she allowed hope back into her heart. Hope of a reconciliation that might one day include Brian.

Back at home she tested the water.

"Well, that was a surprise! Looks like you're going to inherit the house and half the garage!"

"Yes, it's a lovely gesture. I really don't know why we blamed them so harshly for what dad did?"

"I think we were too angry at the way they wanted to tear you away at the time. Perhaps we should have tried harder to mend things while your dad was in prison. I think we just thought they wouldn't want to, after finding out that they weren't even related to you."

Frankie simply shrugged.

Brenda stole herself for the next suggestion.

"I've passed that garage a few times recently though, and it looks almost derelict. I doubt it's going to be worth anything unless someone gets a grip of it!"

"It's not really something we can influence." Frankie sighed as she turned to head for the kitchen.

"Maybe I could do a few hours in the office? You know, see if I can get it back on its feet."

She watched Frankie freeze and hold her position before slowly turning to face her.

"I can't believe you'd even suggest helping that man! He was found guilty of killing my mummy! Guilty remember?"

"I know love, but…"

"There are no buts! Unless my mummy walks back through that fuckin' door, then he's dead to me!"

Brenda was shocked at Frankie's outburst and knew instantly that it was over. She would never lay in Brian's arms again.

Chapter 24

Following the visit, Frankie tried to include the Gilberts in Olivia's life as much as she could.

Brian got a place of his own near to the garage and his absence from their bungalow made contact much easier. At least they got to spoil their Great Granddaughter, their precious Gilly, for a couple of years.

Charlie passed away in the spring of 2017 followed only months later by a devastated Jean.

It was at Jean's funeral that Frankie suspected that her painful, irregular periods and profound bleeding might be an indication of something that could threaten any future childbearing.

During the wake she spent most of the time in a toilet cubicle rolling up wads of tissue to try to prevent the blood from trickling into her shoes.

"You need to see a doctor." Brenda reprimanded when they finally got home.

"I already know what this is." Frankie said coldly. "I know the symptoms. This is fibroids and the only cure is going to be a hysterectomy! My childbearing days are over!"

"It's not as bad as it sounds." Sheila assured as she manoeuvred her walking frame through the lounge door. "Sitting on the couch with paracetamol and a hot water bottle isn't going to cure it! A hysterectomy isn't the end of the world at your age. It's not like you were planning on having another baby!"

Frankie nodded compliantly through her resentment. Maybe Sheila was right. It was too late now for another baby but losing her womb felt suddenly catastrophic. Like the end of her womanhood. The womanhood that never really got started at all.

That night she tried to be positive and take stock of her life. She had Olivia and she had a family of sorts, but none of that made her feel like a real woman.

She'd never really made love with a man nor cooked for one. She'd never even woken up with a man or watched him shave or any of the things associated with being a woman or a wife. Now, it suddenly felt like she never would, and for that reason alone she wanted so badly to keep her womb. The symbol of her womanhood, and her ticket to all those things.

She took more paracetamol and filled many more hot water bottles before she finally relented and went to the doctor for the devastating news, she was sure was about to be delivered.

After an examination she was sent for a scan because the doctor suspected, as she also feared, that she was suffering from numerous fibroids.

"At least you'll get some time off work!" Brenda laughed. "You'll get a very long Christmas break with Olivia."

Olivia immediately jumped onto her lap and scooped her arms around Frankie's neck.

"I know! I know! I'm being silly. It just feels like a huge milestone. Like the opposite of getting your first period and becoming a woman."

"At least you got to use yours!" Brenda laughed again.

"Oh, I'm sorry mum. I didn't think."

"It's fine. I've never felt less of a woman. How could I when I've been a mother in every way that matters. You have done it for real though. You're a woman in every sense of the word."

Frankie's heart sank again. If only Brenda knew the real extent of her missing love life or that the dates she still sometimes pretended to have, were spent alone in cafes or bingo halls.

"I don't think you should be making any plans to move out just yet though." Brenda added.

"Move out? Why would I move out?"

Brenda looked startled. "You've just inherited the Gilberts house! I assumed you and Olivia were intending to move back to the village."

"What!" Frankie exclaimed, "Move out of this den of madness with free childcare and housemaids? Not on your life! This is our home. Right here!"

She watched Brenda's relief seep into her face to cause a huge grin. "I'll help you get it rented out then, shall I?"

"Do what you like with it." Frankie huffed. "I'm keeping it for Olivia's future, not mine. Move dad back into it if you want. I don't care."

Brenda pulled Frankie close.

"I'll come with you for your scan results if you want?" She whispered as she tried to hide her excitement at having an excuse to contact Brian. Her mind was already racing ahead to the prospect of getting him back into his family home and having an ongoing excuse to drop in to check on the property. She shook the thoughts away and smiled.

"When do you get the results? I'll put it in my diary."

"No, its fine." She replied firmly. "It doesn't feel safe to leave Olivia alone with Sheila and Barry anymore. She doesn't always hear very well and he's so unsteady on his legs."

Brenda nodded as she pulled the pin from her silver blonde hair ready to be brushed for bed.

That night, Frankie slid in beside Gilly for the usual bedtime story but as she repeated the sparce text from the floppy over-sized book, her mind started to wander back to her own childhood.

Suddenly, the memory of cuddling up to her own mummy and the old Noddy books came to mind. The memory of those small hard-backed books with their comical pictures and exciting stories. Of Noddy, Bigears and Tubby Bear singing in the little car on their way for an ice cream. She hauled another page over and wondered how this book ever caught a publisher's interest. The sketches might have been drawn by a child and the whole story consisted of no more than a paragraph stretched over a dozen pages. It seemed that storybooks were not what they used to be.

"Storybooks aren't what they used to be." Gilly said suddenly.

Frankie's blood ran cold, and her heart started to pound.

"What made you say that?" She tried to hold her voice steady.

"I don't know." Gilly replied casually as she tried to turn the page Frankie was holding with her thumb staring blankly at the page they had already finished.

She felt Olivia's head turn and realised she'd stopped reading the words, so she smiled, ruffled those curls affectionately and turned the page with a shaking hand.

She cleared her throat and tried to relax but already she could feel the prickle of perspiration dampening her skin.

She forced the bland words from her dry throat, suddenly grateful that the author had been economical with the plot.

"Well, that's the end, love." She smiled as she closed the book and slid out of the bed, grateful for the cooler air on her skin.

"And no-one got an ice cream!" Frankie concluded as she settled down to sleep.

Frankie's legs turned to jelly as she tried to hold the frozen smile on her face and take the few steps towards the door.

She took the stairs two at a time and burst into the living room where Barry, Sheila and Brenda were engrossed in film.

Brenda pressed the pause button immediately on seeing Frankie's expression.

"What is it? Are you alright?"

"Something just happened with Gilly!"

As she retold the sequence of events, her eyes constantly darted from one face to another to detect any spontaneous reaction they may try to hide.

As soon as she'd finished her account, Barry pulled himself up and reached for his walking stick.

"I'm going to leave you all to it." He announced with a nervous cough. "I'd like to say that this doesn't interest me, but the truth is that it scares the crap out of me!"

With that, he ambled his way to the door and disappeared.

Frankie turned to Sheila.

"Come and sit beside me love." She smiled, patting the space in the sofa.

Frankie sat down and for the next hour the two women revealed everything they knew about Olivia's perceived ability to hear the words that had not been spoken.

About Brenda's belief that she'd sensed something was wrong when Frankie was supposed to be on those fake dates with Malcolm and then, after a nod from Sheila, about the thing that started as a game between her and Amelia.

"You used to play a game of mind-reading with my mummy?"

Brenda could see Sheila's eyes warning her not to go any further and consequently she heeded the warning and simply laughed it off. She knew this was not the time to start talking of Amelia's unsettling account of her connection to Frank on the day she vanished. Perhaps there would be a time to spill out the whole unlikely truth but not today when she was already in fear of her own daughter.

"It's just science, really." Brenda comforted. "Like a gift of the brain I suppose. Some people make a living out of it in concert halls!"

"You think its hereditary?" Frankie asked more calmly.

"I think it might be." Brenda replied solemnly "but I don't think its something you'd want to encourage."

This time Frankie caught a glimpse of a covert exchange of eye contact between them and it caused her skin to prickle again. She wasn't sure what that exchange meant but she didn't need telling twice.

"You need to ignore it, Frankie! Do you hear?"

"Yes, I hear you." Frankie smiled as she gave Sheila a hug. "I'll try to pretend it never happened."

"Good girl."

Frankie got up and walked back towards the door.

"It is kind of a nice feeling though, to know I have a special connection with my little girl. Perhaps we'll talk about you in plain sight!"

"Get out of here!" Sheila grinned as she threw a slipper in Frankie's direction.

After she left the room and they heard her footsteps on the stairs, the two women huffed in simultaneous relief at having survived the conversation.

"What are you thinking?" Brenda asked.

"That this thing wasn't something you and Amelia developed between you. I'm thinking that it was always there just as it was with Frank."

"Like a gift?"

"No!" Sheila said harshly. "Like a curse!"

"A curse?" Brenda laughed. "You sound like one of those cackling witches from the dark ages, warning passers by of your future prophets!"

"Well, I'm no prophet, that's for sure but if I had a mind to share my prediction…"

"What?" Sheila had stopped talking to take a breath.

"Well, based on what just happened upstairs, this isn't over. There's more to come. Much more."

Brenda sat silently and Sheila did the same.

"You coming to bed?" Barry asked in a whisper after silently opening the door.

"Yes, I'm coming." Sheila replied.

Brenda stood up at the same time and they both went their separate ways without acknowledging the other.

There was nothing more to be said, because there was nothing they could do, other then to wait and see. To wait and hope that Sheila's prediction was unfounded.

A week later, Frankie sat opposite the doctor dreading the results that might announce the end of her womanhood.

"I'm really sorry, Frankie."

She took a deep breath and prepared herself.

"Don't tell me. Fibroids and a hysterectomy?"

"No, you don't have fibroids."

She felt a hand on her shoulder from behind and turned to see that a nurse had entered the room silently as the doctor continued talking.

"I'm afraid you've contracted something called HPV."

"What's that?"

"It's a virus that is passed on mostly from sexual contact."

"I have an STD!"

"I'm afraid it's more complicated than that Frankie. There are many types of HPV and you have been extremely unlucky in contracting two of the most dangerous strains of it. HPV16 and 18. When did you have your last smear test?"

Frankie was starting to feel hot. Flushed from embarrassment and worried by the doctor's tone.

"Er. I haven't had one since Olivia was born. I got a letter a couple of years ago, but I'd not long been back at work, and I was in the middle of an Ofsted inspection."

She waited for the doctor's reprimand, but it didn't come.

"So, what's the treatment and how long will it take?"

Still, the doctor didn't speak. He didn't speak, he didn't reprimand, and he didn't shake his head disapprovingly. He did none of the things she was expecting.

He smiled weakly and leaned forward a little before speaking in the gentlest voice.

"I don't know yet, about the treatment Frankie but these two viruses have managed to get a firm grip on you and have progressed into something even more dangerous. I'm afraid you have cervical cancer."

Frankie felt the blood drain from her body and down into the floor below. She was no longer listening because she could no longer hear any words. Muffled sounds echoed all around her, but she was no longer a person. No longer human.

She felt the warmth of the woman's arms, but she was still unable to process the events that were happening around her.

Sometime later. Maybe seconds or minutes or hours, a cup of sweet tea was pressed to her lips, and she sipped obediently because there was nothing to do now, other than to obey. She had no ideas or intentions of her own so she could only obey.

She remembered laying down but didn't know for how long and then she smelt the familiar perfume. Suddenly, Brenda was stroking her hair.

"I sent for your mum, Frankie." The doctor said apologetically, as though suddenly realising he should never have delivered such news to someone who had no support at hand.

"Mum?"

"Yes. I'm here. I'm right here, love."

"Olivia?"

"Sheila and a neighbour are watching her. She's fine."

"He said I have cancer mum!"

"I know. I know. But that doesn't mean it's the scary kind!"

She smiled at the doctor as though apologising for Frankie's over-reaction, but he didn't return the smile.

"Perhaps we should go through this when you've all had the chance to get over the shock of it?"

"No." Brenda snapped. "I think we need to talk about it now to put her mind at rest.

Out of the corner o her eye, she saw the doctor shaking his head, but it was too late. Frankie had already grasped the glimmer of hope with both hands.

She swung her legs from the trolly she'd been placed on, and sat up.

"Just tell me about the treatment and how long it will last and how bad the side-effects are going to get. I think I just need to know that, so I can prepare for it."

"I wish is was that simple." The doctor said softly. "But we need to do more tests and scans first. It may be that we attempt to shrink the tumours with chemotherapy and then operate."

Frankie nodded eagerly but Brenda's hand was already stroking her soothingly in a manner she didn't like.

"Am I going to die?"

No-one replied.

Chapter 25

That was the day when everything changed.

When all plans to rent out the Gilbert's house, to make secret contact with Brian, to decorate Olivia's room, to plan meals or shop for food, stopped.

The world had stopped turning. Its axis jolted to a halt with the force of that hung silence of that unanswered question, leaving their world permanently facing the darkness of night. The thick darkness of helplessness, hopelessness, and dread.

Frankie was no longer a teacher, Olivia no longer the bright little torch gleaming with the promise of a happy future and Brenda was no longer the voice of positivity reminding everyone that things would be alright.

As Frankie started her chemotherapy it seemed that the family had been stunned into silence. Holding its breath until some delivery of positive news would allow it to blow out and start to breathe again.

Brenda knew it was her job to hold up her daughter with dogged optimism, but she was barely dragging herself from one day to the next. It felt like the whole family had already accepted the inevitable and had numbed themselves for the downhill journey into the abyss.

As ever, it was to be Sheila's enormous strength that would eventually creak their world back into motion and turn it slowly back towards daylight.

They had been sat watching tv, when an advertisement for a summer holiday suddenly filled the screen with images of happy families running through the waves on a sunny beach.

Brenda suddenly slammed down her teacup and stormed from the room.

Sheila smiled at Frankie comfortingly and followed her into the kitchen.

"We can't go on like this Bren. I know it's hard, but we can't just curl up and die. Frankie needs us right now. All of us."

"No!" Brenda snapped. "What Frankie needs is a future. We all do. Did you see that stupid advert? Idiots! People acting like they are going to live forever and dance in the sun with everyone they ever loved. It's all a lie! A big fat lie! We're all fools! Everyone of us because sooner or later the heartbreak will come. The bubble will burst, and we'll see how stupidly we allowed a moment of happiness to deceive us!"

"Oh love." Sheila soothed as she pulled Brenda into her arms and stroked back the silver hair in exactly the same way as she used to stroke the silky blonde curls of childhood. Closing her eyes, she tried to give her inner strength to the little girl she remembered. Just as she had when Brenda had been teased at school or failed a maths test.

"You have to give whatever Frankie needs now."

"What Frankie needs is time," Brenda sobbed, "and I can't give her that!"

"Life is short, love," Sheila whispered, "but I don't think death is the end. I really don't and what we do now is just as important as everything else we have done so far. Those adverts are not there to deceive us but to encourage us to make the most of the joy while we are here. To make memories we can take to our old age and beyond."

"I wish I had your faith." Brenda whispered back.

"The only faith you need, Bren, is in yourself. In your strength and determination to support the daughter you inherited from your sister. She needs your stupid humour and strength more than she's ever needed it before. You need to dig deep now. For Frankie, for Olivia and for Amelia. Can you do that?"

She felt Brenda sigh.

"Can you?"

Brenda pulled away and nodded.

"Yes, I can do that."

"Louder!"

Brenda grinned and as that grin broke onto her face, she wondered how they would ever have survived if her father hadn't dragged her back into his life.

They returned to the living room and Brenda switched off the tv.

"Anyone fancy a game of charades?"

Oliver clapped her hands. At three years old she had little concept of what her grandma had suggested but she had definitely caught on to the sudden change of mood and that, in itself, was worth a clap and a squeal.

Brenda nodded her gratitude to Sheila.

This was her chance to step up and make a difference regardless of the outcome. There was a battle to be fought and she was going to fight it with everything she had.

Barry pulled the curly-haired little girl onto his knee and squeezed her tight.

"Look at you! I'm sure you've grown since this morning!"

Olivia measured her tiny hand against Barry's and frowned. "Not big as you."

"No. Not yet but you will be! If you hurry up!"

It had been a casual, throw-away joke but it pierced the heart of everyone in that room. The race to get little Gilly, to adulthood, was on because if anything was to happen to Frankie, Olivia would be left in the care of the elderly. Every one of them descending into their twilight years as the infant pushed her way through their crumbling existence like the only green shoot of life in a dying meadow.

The lonely green shoot that would need to dig deep for its instincts of survival and with the dogged determination of mother nature, she would fight for her own existence regardless of the consequences, or the lonely unsupported life she would face.

Frankie had given birth a generation later than most and the consequence was right there in that room. The gap in their succession that could leave Olivia without a fit, capable, energetic person to nurture her into adulthood.

No-one said it out loud but each of them instantly realised the importance of surviving the next twenty years with their bodies and faculties intact. None more so than Frankie. She had to survive this!

As her hair thinned, she cut it from waist length to shoulder and tied it in a ponytail to disguise the bald patches.

"Where's your pretty hair?" Olivia asked the moment she walked into the room.

"I cut it off. Don't you like it?"

"No!" Olivia said stubbornly. "It's not pretty anymore."

Brenda shook her head and smiled but Frankie was already fighting the first of many tears to come.

"I'm going to start the Christmas shopping soon." Brenda blurted to change the subject. "You need to write your letter to Santa, Gilly. Is there a toy you would like?"

Olivia didn't yet understand the whole concept, but she liked any sentence containing the word toy.

"I want a dolly with long hair!"

"Well, let's write the letter then." Brenda smiled, ignoring the connection to Frankie's lost locks.

Frankie watched the scene unfold as pens and paper emerged. The letter to Santa was written on the floor between Brenda and Olivia while Sheila and Barry made independent list of everything they needed for the perfect Christmas.

Barry was planning a full-blown snow scene of reindeers and lights on the front driveway and Sheila was planning a banquet fit for a king.

As she toyed with her thin ponytail and watched her little girl try to draw a doll amidst the scribbles of a letter, she felt her stomach tighten. It tightened from the physical pain that her medication suddenly seemed unable to calm, but it tightened also from the recognition of the scene before her.

This was not the family she knew planning their Christmas just as they always had. This was the rallying of her family pulling out all the stops. Without even realising it, they were all sending a message loud and clear that they didn't think she was going to see another one. These lists and excited plans had the words 'wake' and 'last supper' written all over them.

She didn't speak of it, or of the panic it was reeking in her tightened chest. But, as she watched them scribbling enthusiastically, they might as well have been pumping up the satin pillows in her coffin. Her chest was now so tight that she could barely breathe.

"Are you alright?" Sheila asked. Suddenly noticing the expression on her face.

"Yes. Yes, I'm fine."

Frankie tried to take deep, slow breaths. These were the people she loved most in the world, and they meant well. There was no way she was about to throw cold water over their kindness. Sometimes, she concluded, you must accept love in whatever misguided form it is given. She just wished their lists were of the usual cheap crackers from Poundland, wrapping paper from the market and a frozen Turkey from Iceland. A list like that would have given her far more comfort and confidence that she was expected to survive.

On the run up to Christmas Frankie found herself feeling more and more nervous. She wished she could speak her mind to someone, to anyone, but she couldn't bear to inflict her fear and devastation on the well-meaning hearts that had gone to so much effort.

How could she possibly tell them that they were making her feel like the condemned man? That, as Christmas day approached, she was feeling more and more terrified.

She wondered how any condemned man could ever have ordered his last meal of choice and managed to swallow it because her own throat was already closed with dread. She remembered visiting an old prison once and being told tales of highwaymen who had ordered huge steaks and eggs for breakfast before stepping onto the gallows!

Now, as she arranged the gold luxury crackers onto the new silk tablecloth on Christmas eve, she concluded that those were braver times, or maybe just of greater faith. Times when everyone believed, without doubt, that the hangman's rope was about to open the gate to a new beginning. A new life. How else could they have stepped onto the gallows with a full belly and a hearty wave to the crowd?

She straightened the cutlery and wished with all her heart that she shared their faith. She wished the pain in her lower back would go away and she wished the ache in her heart would dissolve and allow her to feel joy again. Just for one day.

She went upstairs and peeped in on Olivia. Her mass of brown curls sprawled over her pink pillow as she slept contentedly with her mouth open and a delicate snore rhythmically counting down the seconds to Christmas morning.

She stood in the doorway committing the scene to memory. A memory that would comfort her in her darkest moments, raise a smile of gratitude in her desolation and hopefully stay with her forever, in this life or in the next.

She closed the door quietly and went to her room to lay out the Christmas jumper and reindeer ears to remind her in the morning that she was going to be full of Christmas joy. One way or another!

Next morning, the outfit did the trick.

Little Gilly sat on her knee and tugged on her antlers, and everyone laughed as she opened her gifts and squealed with delight.

Frankie had set the tone and she had done it well. Everyone followed her lead, and the room was filled with good humour and, to an onlooker, undisputable Christmas joy.

Like a confident Colonel, she had led her regiment into battle with a bold heart and a buoyant guise and they had taken the torch swiftly from her hand and marched forward with its radiant flame. Now she could fall back through the ranks and take her place in the tranquillity of the sofa while she watched the day unfold.

Everyone else would remember that Christmas as a wonderful fun-filled day.

Frankie would remember it as her gift of gratitude to the family she loved.

In January she returned to Rochdale infirmary for the operation to remove her tumours. She didn't dare to hope for the best but deep inside she prayed with all her might for God to give her this one thing.

The chance to bring up her beloved daughter.

She closed her eyes on the face of a masked nurse and opened them on the homely, smiling face of the woman who had been by her side for most of her life.

Brenda stroked her bald head and wrinkled her nose in greeting.

"How are you feeling love?"

Frankie tried to speak but her throat was dry and sore from the anaesthetic.

Instantly, Brenda reached for the plastic cup and slid her hand behind Frankie's neck to help her take a sip.

Frankie swallowed greedily and then tried again to speak.

"How did it go? Did they get it? All of it?"

"No-one has been to see us yet." Brenda comforted. "I'm sure the doctor will come in now you're awake. I'll go and find out."

Brenda disappeared and left Frankie to ponder these indescribable moments. Moments heavy and thick with dread and hope. Seesawing mercilessly in waves. An unprecedented brand of sickly excitement and anticipation. Unbearable yet treasured. Hated yet loved for its uncertainty. The last moments before the ball settled on red or black.

She closed her eyes to both savour and endure them as she prayed again.

The scrape of a chair caused her to reopen them at the unfamiliar face of the white-coated surgeon.

"I'm afraid.."

She didn't need to hear the remainder of his sentence. It was irrelevant now. The ball had settled on black!

Brenda was the only person listening to the words that formed the drole of noise Frankie could make no sense of.

"I'm afraid we couldn't remove the tumour because it had spread into surrounding tissue and into the bowl and liver."

Brenda reached for Frankie's hand, but it was numb and lifeless.

She turned to the surgeon to demand some glimmer of hope.

"But there are still things you can do? Treatments you can give her to get rid of it?"

The man glanced at Brenda momentarily and then turned his face back to the blank stare of his patient.

"We can talk more about this later. But for now, I think Frankie needs some time to absorb this."

"How long?" Frankie said suddenly. "How long have I got."

Brenda butted in.

"Don't be talking like that! No-one is giving up here!"

"A couple of weeks. A month at the most. It's hard to predict because this has been ravaging your body so quickly" The man sighed as he watched his words massacre yet another hopeful soul. It had been the third in only a week he had delivered this speech and it was taking its toll. This was the part of his job that he dreaded. This was another face that would haunt him for years to come.

"I thought this kind of cancer moved much more slowly?" Frankie asked.

"It usually does but do you remember all the illnesses you had after you gave birth? Your doctor put on your notes that you had a compromised immune system and that gave the disease the opportunity to really get a hold and to spread far more quickly."

She simply nodded and pulled her hand from under Brenda's, only to replace it on top and smile.

"It's ok mum. At least we know what we are facing now."

As Brenda sobbed, she felt Frankie's hand stroking her hair and had never been prouder of the little girl she had raised through so much adversity.

Frankie didn't deserve this!

God could go fuck himself!

Chapter 26

The next conversation Brenda had with Frankie was to shake her to the core.

It took place two days after the delivery of the devastating news that her future treatment would be purely palliative.

"I'm not coming back home, mum." She announced after Brenda had tried to lighten the mood by telling her about a painting Olivia had done for her.

"Of course, you're coming home!" She retorted. "Home is where you are loved and where you'll be cared for the best."

"And that's exactly why I can't go back there. It would be too hard. Too emotional and too painful. It will be easier on all of us if we don't put ourselves through it." She then pulled herself upright and folded her arms resolutely. "I'm staying here unless I'm forced into a hospice."

"But what about Gilly?"

"Olivia will be better off this way."

Brenda noticed how quickly Frankie had reverted to her daughter's formal name. Already, she was distancing herself emotionally from her own child.

"Surely, you want to see her again. Hold her close again and tell her how much you love her? Surely you do!"

Frankie smiled as she shook her head.

"This is not about what I want, it's about what my child needs from me and what she needs from me right now is to get the hell out of her mind. Out of her heart and out of her life. The sooner she forgets me the sooner she will feel secure again."

She then took a huge deep breath and continued.

"I want you to hide all the photos of me, to distract her if she asks about me, get rid of all my clothes and belongings. Wipe me from her life as completely and cleanly as possible. It's the kindest thing I can do for her now. And for you. All of you."

Brenda was frantically searching for a counterattack. For an argument that would challenge and refute Frankie's words but there were none. Everything she wanted to do for Frankie, taking her home, caring for her and reuniting her with little Gilly would benefit one person only and that person was now being the strongest most selfless person she'd ever encountered.

The harsh reality was that none of them wanted to witness the daily demise of their Frankie. None of them wanted to see that final hug between her and little Gilly. The devastating truth was that they all wanted to be spared from every heart-wrenching second that now lay before them.

"You know I'm right. There's nothing you can do for me now and going back home would hurt me just as much as you. There's nothing left for me now. My happiness is long gone. All I can do now is to stay here and at least to feel the warmth of knowing that you are rebuilding your lives. That's the only glimmer of happiness in front of me and I need it."

Brenda could see that Frankie's mind was made up, but she couldn't bring herself to agree to such abandonment and selfishness. Deep down she knew that the road ahead would be unbearable and if she was completely honest with herself, she was dreading every tortuous moment of it. Frankie was right. They all wanted it to be over so they could start to recover, rebuilt, and eventually to heal.

"We'll talk again tomorrow." She said stubbornly.

Frankie simply shrugged until Brenda picked up her bag and left.

She held back the tears as her mum left and then lay alone in that room and closed her eyes.

She wished her dad was here to comfort her the way he used to when she was a child. His long arms would wrap around her and instantly she felt protected from the world. Then her mind drifted even further back. Back to days when the touch of her real mother's hand would melt away her fears as gently and completely as the first rays of sunshine on a frozen meadow. In her mind she was now a five-year-old child with her mother's hand holding her soul in its curled fingers. The comfort of it was still tangible as she recalled that absolute contentment far beyond anything her dad could create with his wisdom and sound advice. This was something else entirely. The kind of protection only a mother can give when she puts her entire being between her child and harm. What she wouldn't give to feel that just one more time. Just for a moment in her hour of need. She was no longer a woman but a child again, a poorly child, and all she craved was to have her mummy by her side. Just one more touch of her mother's hand.

She opened her eyes and stared at the sterile ceiling as numbness gave way to desperation and to the vain hope that there had been some strand of truth in the suspected hereditary connection between her and Olivia, between Brenda and Amelia and more importantly that it also existed between her and her mummy.

Gently she closed her eyes again to muster every ounce of her strength. She felt the pressure building inside. This was her last chance. Suddenly she screamed with all her being into a place that lay far beyond that hospital ceiling. Somewhere out in the vast unknown she prayed to God that her mother would finally hear her plea.

"Mummy! Mummy! Where are you. Please come back. I need you. Mummy! Mummy! Come back! Please! Please!"

She screamed over and over until her body could no longer bear the strain of it and then she felt a hand on her brow and the reassuring voice of a nurse muttering.

"I'll go and bring her back. She won't have got far."

Frankie realised the misconception and caught the nurse by the hand.

"No. It's fine. I think I was just having a nightmare." She whispered between shallow breaths.

The nurse nodded sympathetically and went about her duties.

Frankie then wiped away her tears and picked up a magazine. Brenda continued her journey home and Sheila sat dozing in her room. None of them remotely aware of the momentous event that had just taken place.

Brenda opened the front door and poked her head into Sheila's room.

"Everything ok?"

"Yes. Barry's faffing about with the hose pipe and Gilly is dancing for me to this awful music."

Gilly instantly beamed and ran into Brenda's arms.

"Where's mummy?"

"Would you like a chocolate biscuit when I bring granny Sheila a cup of tea?"

"Yes please." Olivia smiled as she returned to the rug that had been her stage.

Brenda quietly closed the door and headed for the kitchen with a sinking feeling in the pit of her stomach.

Despite her avid opposition she was already complying with Frankie's wish. She had just distracted Olivia from the subject of her mother. Soon she would stop asking and then she would stop wondering and finally she would stop remembering.

As she waited for the kettle to boil, she heard a knock on the door.

She walked back into the hallway to see Olivia already running to open it.

"You go back in with granny Sheila and wait for your biscuit." She said as she guided Olivia back towards the bedroom door.

Whoever was calling was likely to make some reference to Frankie and whatever it was, she didn't want Olivia to hear it.

She could see the silhouette of a young woman through the glass as she opened the door and stared at that face.

"Mealy?"

"Brenda?"

Chapter 27

Back up in the bedroom, Brenda checked her watch to find that it had been over two hours now since she'd left Amelia and Sheila alone to talk while she cradled Olivia in her arms, and suddenly none of it felt right.

She couldn't leave Sheila to bear the burden alone. It was her place to be by her sister's side not hiding upstairs like a selfish coward.

Slowly she disentangled herself from Olivia and crept back down the stairs. Barry was in the living room with a glass of whisky but there wasn't a sound from the bedroom he shared with Sheila.

"I guess you know what's happened?"

Barry nodded and spoke in an unsettled whisper.

"Have you seen her? She's the same bloody age as the day she left. I don't like this one bit."

He swigged the remnants of his glass and instantly poured himself another.

Brenda walked quietly over the hall and slowly opened the door.

Sheila was still in her chair, sombre and expressionless. Amelia was sitting on the bed with her head in her hands. Motionless.

"Mealy?" She whispered.

Slowly Amelia lifted her head until her reddened eyes met Brenda's and tried to force the words out.

"Frankie's dying?" She croaked "My Frankie? My little girl is dying?"

Brenda folded her arms around her sister's head and pulled her into her stomach, feeling her pain, then feeling her own guilt for so many follies. For not protecting Frankie well enough, for her relationship with Brian and for the resentment she'd harboured over Amelia's perceived abandonment.

There was too much to say. Too many arguments to be had and too many regrets to apologise for, so all that could be done was to hold each other close and allow the tangled jumble of emotions to flow between them until there was nothing left to feel.

"I need to see her. I need to go to her. Right now."

"I'm not sure that's a good idea." Brenda replied gently. "Perhaps in a few days when I've had chance to talk to her."

"Do you even know that she has a few days?" Amelia snapped. "It sounds like this thing could snatch her away at any moment."

Brenda couldn't argue.

"You want to go right away? Right this minute?"

Amelia's face hardened into a determined stare.

"I was there to hold her hand as she came into this world, and I will damn well be there to hold her hand when she leaves it."

Sheila nodded to Brenda.

"You go with her. We'll watch Olivia."

Obediently, Brenda opened the door for Amelia who marched purposefully through it, into the hallway but as she took the car keys from the hook, Amelia started to shake. Her whole body began to tremble until she slid to the floor banging her forehead with her hand and screaming.

Immediately Brenda was down on her knees rocking her back and forth until her body became still again.

"Bren." She said suddenly. "Frankie was sitting beside me on the bus at lunchtime! A few minutes later she was at a sleepover and now…now you're telling me she's in her forties and dying. My God! My God! My God!"

Brenda rocked her again. Back and forth, shushing her like an injured child, kissing the top of her head and trying to absorb some of the pain.

"Perhaps we should leave this until you've had some sleep at least Mealy?"

"No. No, I want to do this now. I need to do it now. I want to see my little girl. My Frankie."

Brenda nodded and held Amelia's hand tightly. For so many years she'd dreamed of her sister's return, and this was nothing like the joyous reunion she'd envisaged. Nothing like the fantasy that had comforted her through the lonely hours when sleep refused to take pity on her.

Amelia's agony had become hers as she tried to absorb the awful, incredible truth that throughout those years of torture, her sister had been only yards away, sleeping in some imaginary or unworldly car of her own making.

She wished she could dispute it. Rage at Mealy for playing the victim with her lies but the truth was seeping through every pore of her sister's body. Shining brightly on that youthful face with its firm jawline, baby-smooth eyelids and taut unblemished flesh. Rising from that awful coat with the same musty aroma of years gone by.

Suddenly Brenda was sharing more than her sister's pain and sorrow, more than her bewilderment and disbelief. Like the unexpected blow of a sledgehammer, emotion had been annihilated by pure terror.

Amelia felt the change and looked up.

Young face to old and old face to young. They did nothing, said nothing. The image before each of them was being silently absorbed and telling its own story of undeniable truth. There was no need for words because something far stronger was a play. This was no time to fall apart.

A few miles away, Frankie was laying quietly with her eyes closed listening to the sounds of the busy ward. The frivolous voices of nurses talking of meaningless issues, oblivious to the terrifying reality of their own mortality. All around them people were dying on this ward yet still they seemed impervious to it, or to the fact that their time would come, and probably as suddenly and unexpectedly as her own. She couldn't decide if they were exceptionally brave or just plain stupid as they concerned themselves with an affair on Coronation Street, speculated on who might win the match on Saturday and cursed whoever had put all the wet spoons back in the sugar bowl on the tea trolley!

It made her both angry and sad at the same time. Part of her wanted to shake them but part of her wanted to hug them because, in so many ways, they reminded her of spring lambs playing in the meadow. Lambs full of the joy, warmth and pleasure this world has to offer as they leapt and frolicked only yards away from the slaughter shed.

She breathed in deeply and tried to block out the sounds of the lives that were unaffected by her situation, immune to her dread and terror and would barely blink when she turned quietly from person to corpse.

Then suddenly yet slowly it came. The strangely familiar scent of something from long ago. She couldn't place it, but she recognised it and wondered if this was the start of it all. The start of the flashbacks of life that so many people believed in. As it grew in strength it seemed to force open her eyes with the enormous impact of that musty scent. She blinked against the light and there it was. The face from a thousand photographs that she'd thumbed and stroked for over thirty years!

"Mummy?"

The face smiled and instantly changed to another photograph she'd cherished.

"Mummy. It that you?"

She didn't need to hear the answer because, as the tears trickled down that face, she felt something surge through her body.

That touch of that hand hit her like a thunderbolt. This was the touch she remembered. The touch of her mother's hand on hers leaving her in no doubt that she was home. Everything was going to be alright now because her mummy had got her and if her mother was an angel here to collect her, she was ready to go gladly and unafraid.

"Yes. It's me. I'm here darling. I'm here now."

Brenda could barely breathe as she watched the beautiful, heart-wrenching reunion of mother and daughter. Painful, almost horrific yet still the most beautiful moment she would ever witness, and somewhere deep inside she felt a sense of relief at finally handing back her parental responsibility to its rightful owner.

Frankie turned to see Brenda's tears and reality struck. Brenda could see her mummy too. This was no angel. This was a living person. Her mummy had come back alive!

The shock of it, the joy of it and the dread of it collided in mid-air before they hit her simultaneously.

Her mummy was alive. Her mummy was back. Her mummy was not here to guide her into the next life but to watch her leave this life alone.

She searched the faces around her for some shred of comfort but there was none. This was a journey she must make on her own and the two women who had jointly protected her would be waving her off as helplessly as they had on her first day at school.

Fear and panic descended until she could barely breathe. She gasped for air as terror constricted her chest until there was no strength left to fight for it, but then something miraculous happened.

Amelia's arms folded around her, and her breathing returned to normal. The reassurance and comfort of her mummy travelled through every nerve of her body as she allowed herself to sink into the arms that had been the first to hold her. The first and probably the last.

Mother and daughter held each other close for the longest time in complete silence as though drawing strength from the other, healing the wounds of time and rejoining their souls to face the ordeal ahead.

After several minutes, Frankie was the first to break that divine silence.

"My dad didn't hurt you!"

"No, he didn't." Amelia croaked. "Your dad would never do that."

"Where have you been then? Why didn't you come home?"

Brenda sat silently while Amelia tried to describe her own version of what was, to her, one awful, terrifying, incredulous day.

"Are you seriously asking me to believe that you haven't been anywhere!"

Amelia simply maintained eye contact with her daughter.

"Honestly? That only this morning you think you and I were sitting in the Wimpey bar with that rainbow dress?"

Amelia didn't flinch. Her eyes remained steady and steadfast.

"Oh my God. You're telling the truth! You are, aren't you?"

Amelia nodded and then stroked her daughters bald head again.

"I'm afraid I am, and I'm as terrified as you, right now. Your dad didn't do anything to me love. I don't know what's happened, but I do know that."

Even amid the trauma of everything else she was hearing, Frankie recognised this as her last chance to reconcile with her wonderful dad and she reached for it.

"Can I see him? I would really like to see him."

"Of course, you can." Amelia forced a smiled. "Sheila told me what he did but I don't blame him. I know he didn't intend to kill Frank. He just lashed out because I was planning to break up our family. I was the one to blame here."

Frankie pushed herself up on the pillow slightly, grimacing against the pain.

"I can't take this in. I really can't. I feel like I'm in a gigantic nightmare. All these years! Why now?

Amelia stroked her again.

"I thought you'd called me and woken me up. I heard you call me. Frankie. I heard your voice."

Frankie started to cry.

"Why didn't I do that right away? After you left? I could have called for you and you could have come back while I was still a little girl! Why didn't I! Why didn't I!"

"None of this is your fault." Amelia started to cry too. "This was all my fault. Mine! Do you hear me? I started this with my mind-reading tricks and then my plot to steal you away from your dad."

"Why? Why were you going to do that?"

Amelia sighed heavily. She didn't need to try to remember because it had been only a few hours ago.

"There are different kinds of love, Frankie but I suppose you already know that. The love I have for the dad you knew was a very gentle love but sometimes a different kind of love takes you in it's wake and refuses to let you go."

"I don't understand."

Brenda instantly felt the pang of Frankie's reply. She was lying there in the claws of death without ever having felt either kind of love that her mother was describing.

"It's more like a compulsion." Amelia continued. "Some sort of fever that takes you in its fist and refuses to give you a moment of peace. A craving deep inside that torments your heart. It's almost an addiction."

Frankie shrugged her ignorance of it.

"I was being selfish, Frankie. That's the top and bottom of it. I'll ask auntie Brenda to go and find him. I'm sure she'll know where he is."

There was a look from Amelia that Brenda recognised instantly. A knowing look. She then smiled and knew that Sheila had told her everything. She knew about her relationship with Brian, and she had already forgiven it.

Brenda squeezed Amelia's hand in gratitude and left the ward to seek out Brian with a new urgency in her heart.

As she pulled up outside his new address, she sat for a moment to prepare herself.

How cruelly fate had delivered her the opportunity she'd been longing for. So many years she'd wasted, hoping and praying, for Amelia's return to vindicate Brian. To repair the mistrust between the two people who meant everything to her. For the door to open again and allow her to fall back into his long bony arms and return her to the happiest times of her life.

She cursed God for the second time that month. For his warped sense of humour or his cruel way of teaching her to appreciate what she had.

If he existed at all then he had taught her well because as she sat in that car and looked at the flickering of the tv lights in Brian's window there was not an ounce of passion or lust left in her.

Right now, she would trade this man, and her sister for the life she had a few months ago. For the opportunity to bring up little Gilly with Frankie, Sheila, and Barry by her side. She had been blessed. Truly blessed but too greedy or stupid to allow contentment to nestle in her heart.

She turned off the engine and made her way up the path towards the small row of steps to his front door.

"Bren!" Brian's face turned grey.

"Is it Frankie? I heard about her illness. Is it our little girl? Has she gone?"

Brian was already crying, and Brenda's tears fell instantly at the sheer impact of seeing his love, bubble over so unreservedly.

All she could do was to shake her head.

"What then? What is it Bren?"

Brenda opened her mouth, drew in a gulp of air and blew it back out again.

"She wants to see you, Brian. She is very weak. She hasn't got long but she wants to see you."

Brenda felt the impact of Brian's body as he hurtled by her, tripping down the steps and landing in a ball on the path. He jumped back up and stared at her with a blooded chin.

"What you waiting for!"

Brenda looked down at his feet.

"You're going to need shoes."

As Brian dashed back into the house for shoes, she contemplated that, under any other circumstances, they would both be rolling around in a fit of uncontrollable laughter but today their hearts were too full of desperation, emotion, dread and love. There was no space for even a morsel of humour.

As she drove, she tried to think of a way of delivering the next unbelievable piece of news. There was no way of softening the blow so, as she pulled back into the hospital carpark and opened the door, she simply said the words.

"Amelia's back."

She heard Brian drop back onto the passenger seat.

"What?"

"You heard me."

"When? How?"

Brenda stood beside the car with her keys jangling as he got back onto his feet.

"Bren! What happened?"

Brenda fidgeted for a moment and then looked right at him.

"She just walked up to my door and rang the fuckin bell! Don't ask me where she's been or how she got back but it's exactly like before."

"She came back with milk?"

This time Brenda couldn't suppress an involuntary giggle. Despite the horrific, heartrending situation he'd somehow, stupidly managed to invoke a moment of humour. Shamefully she got it under control in an instant, feeling both dammed and saved by it. This man was her only hope of surviving this.

"No! She didn't bring bloody milk," she snapped, "she just walked in and said she'd only been gone for three hours! My head's a fuckin shed Brian! I don't know what's going on?"

"Well, obviously she's making it up. Probably got herself another family somewhere and thought she'd turn up for a bit of inheritance or something. Maybe she heard of my parents' deaths?"

As he caught up with her, she stopped and turned to face him.

"Brian. She's not been anywhere. She's still in the same clothes and she's still twenty-two years old!"

As she marched across the carpark, she could hear that Brian had remained where she'd left him. Rooted to the spot, staring at the image of her marching away.

She turned and took pity on him.

As she slowly walked back towards him, he slowly moved forward to close the gap.

She reached out her hands, and he took them. Drawing her close until she was back inside those huge arms again with her face buried in his neck.

Just like Frankie and Amelia, they were reconnecting. Re-bonding and preparing themselves to face whatever came next.

Chapter 28

Frankie's eyes jerked open to the sound of three chairs clattering over the floor.

Brian had caught his heel around the metal leg of one and the others had zigzagged behind like hand-locked unruly children.

"Dad." She smiled.

"Hi Princess," he smiled back tearily, "I hear you've got yourself in a bit of a pickle?"

"You could say that." She continued to smile. This was a moment she'd been hoping for most of her life. She hadn't set eyes on that wonderful ugly face since she was eleven years old and seeing it now, aged and weathered, he looked strangely handsome. Her smile remained, as she sighed. Time had a way of somehow balancing things, redistributing beauty until everyone looked somehow equal in appearance. She looked over at Brenda who was still a remarkably handsome woman but her slightly sagging jaw and crows' feet had brought her more in line with Brian. No-one would call them Beauty and the Beast in the way they used to when she was at school. They now seemed a perfectly matched couple.

She was still holding her mother's hand and felt a sudden pang of guilt as she realised that she considered Brenda and Brian to be a couple. Her parents. It all seemed such a mess. She remembered Brian as her dad from being a toddler to his arrest, yet she seemed incapable of processing the changeover between Amelia and Brenda as her mum, the other parent. It had all happened so suddenly yet so seamlessly. She sighed again and felt the instantaneous response in a squeeze from the hand that still held hers. The hand of her real mother.

Amelia could sense the tension of it and spoke directly to Frankie but allowing Brian and Brenda to overhear.

"Life is strange, Frankie and ours has been even stranger. I loved your biological daddy with all my heart, but I married a different man because it was the best thing to do at the time. The dad you knew. This funny, lovely man behind me. I learned to love him, and he learned to love me because I gave him the chance to be a husband and a dad. We did love each other for a while but it was never the kind of love I had for Frank." She waited a second before adding, "or the kind of love he has for auntie Brenda, and she has for him."

She then released Frankie's hand for a moment and walked towards them as they stood side by side in front of the mangle of chairs.

For a moment, Brian was rooted to the spot by the spectacle before him. The same wife who had escaped from her bed a lifetime ago! Every inch of her frozen in time. The colours and blemishes of her complexion, the length and texture of her hair, the way she moved and spoke. All the things he had forgotten had been perfectly preserved!

She raised her arms and hooked them around each of them and pulled them in.

"I love you both. I'm grateful to you both and you deserve to have some happiness at last. Together."

"But I..." Brian stammered.

"Yes, you killed the love of my life, but I know you didn't mean to, and I know I was cruel and selfish towards you. If you had been planning to rip Frankie from my life and put another woman in my place as her mother, I think I might have hit her with a crowbar myself."

"A wrench." Brian corrected.

Everyone stared at him for a moment and then laughed out loud. Brian had done it again. Brought laughter into the darkest of places and the three women of his life relished the relief of it whole-heartedly.

The ice of decades had been broken by the family clown.

"Can I have some time alone with mum?" Frankie asked when the giggles had subsided.

Amelia and Brenda exchanged a glance.

"Sorry, I mean with this mum." She explained as she regained Amelia's hand.

"Of course, darling." Frankie smiled.

"First can I give my little girl a hug? I've been saving it up for so many years." Brian interrupted.

Gently he folded his arms around her shoulders, lifting her slightly from her pillow as his lips kissed her patchy balding head. Only a few random strands of the beautiful black mane remained. Stubborn strands that refused to abandon her. He stroked them gratefully for their effort to remind the world what a stunning beauty his little girl had been.

"I brought you something." He whispered as he kissed her cheek and gently lowered her back to the support of her pillow.

He reached into his jacket pocket and produced a bundle of letters.

"These are not all of them. I threw away a few hundred but kept the most important ones." He smiled. "I wrote far too many, but I didn't have much else to do inside."

"You didn't send them?"

"No. Everyone believed I'd killed your mum. I thought they'd got more chance of being read if I held onto them until she returned. I thought if I sent them from prison, you'd most likely wipe your arse on them."

Frankie instantly held her stomach to counteract the spasm of laughter.

"I've missed you so much dad."

Her words flooded his eyes instantly. For a moment they held hands and allowed the desolation of those wasted years to be processed. Each of them soaking up the regret, remorse, and the sheer sorrow of it until the inevitable, mandatory crumb of acceptance allowed their hands to loosen and separate.

Amelia took the letters and placed them on the table.

"I'll read them to her later."

Brian nodded, wiped the snot over his face with the back of his hand and returned to Brenda who was standing with the door ajar.

Amelia sat back down beside the bed as Brenda and Brian left.....hand in hand.

"You look exhausted." Amelia said gently. "Why don't you take a nap and I'll stay right here until you wake up."

"I don't think I dare, mummy."

Amelia felt instantly shocked that her little girl still spoke to her as a five-year-old would. The five-year-old she'd walked out on only this morning. The morning that was now 37 years ago!

"I think it will be fine if you had a little sleep, love."

"I don't want to sleep."

"Ok. So, what do you want?"

Frankie's expression hardened.

"I want to read every one of those letters, I want to take Gilly to her first day at school, I want to play chess with dad again, I want to pull a cracker on Christmas day." She took a breath to blow away the emotion that might steal her ability to talk. "I want time, and you can't give me that."

Amelia felt like she'd been sprayed with a machine gun. Every bullet of a wish had pounded her body and her heart was aching with the weight of her own helplessness.

There was nothing she could do to grant her daughter's wishes but there was something she could share that would take away some of the pain of it.

"No, I can't give you more time here, but I can perhaps give you hope of a future."

"A future? I have no future."

As she stroked those stubborn, loyal strands of hair she spoke gently and quietly to her daughter of those moments with Frank.

Of the ten minutes and the three hours that had stolen her life. Of her moments with a dead man. A dead man who was still talking to her!

She told her story without interruption, without taking in her surroundings or wating for a reaction. As though she was reliving every precious, terrifying moment of it. The moments that had taken place only hours earlier.

As she finished with the moment that she'd knocked on the door of the new house that she and Brenda had envied, she came out of her trance-like recollection expecting to find Frankie fast asleep, but what she saw in that bed caused her to gasp.

Frankie was sitting bolt upright with her legs swung off the bed and her face only a foot away from her mother's. Her eyes wide and alive, her hands clenched and still.

Frankie had been drinking in every morsel of her mother's emotional recollection.

"Frankie, are you alright?"

Frankie took her hand.

"Is this the truth mum? Is it the truth?"

"Yes, it's the truth. The terrible fucked-up truth."

"You're telling me that in this place. This weird place somewhere between the dead and the living that time is somehow different?"

"Yes, I am. I think time just passes more slowly there. That every year here is equivalent to just five minutes. I sat with Frank for just five minutes the first time and when I went back to that lane, I just fell asleep with exhaustion."

"And that was for three hours?"

"Yes, it was, and I would probably have been there even longer if I hadn't had a dream that you were calling for me!"

Frankie felt her blood run cold.

"What did I call?"

"I dreamt you were shouting - Mummy! Mummy! Where are you. Please come back. I need you. Mummy! Mummy! Come back!"

She looked over at Frankie who had suddenly started to shake. An alarm sounded on her monitor and a nurse rushed in.

"Her heart rate is off the scale! What happened?"

"I don't know!" Amelia gasped. "Is she going to be alright?"

The nurse settled her down and took her pulse as the monitor stopped blaring and Frankie's heart rate returned to normal.

"Where's her mum?"

Amelia swallowed her urge to correct the woman and smiled.

"She's just nipped home to attend to Frankie's daughter, but I'll be staying."

"You want to stay all night? Are you a relative."

"Yes." Frankie interrupted. "She is a relative and she's staying."

A cot bed was then brought into the room and the nurse asked to speak to Amelia outside.

"I think maybe her mother ought to come back tomorrow."

Amelia could read the message in the nurse's tone.

"You think she hasn't got long?"

"It's hard to say but her vital signs are deteriorating faster than expected so I just thought that maybe she should make sure she spends as much time here as possible?"

"I'll let her know." Amelia nodded.

Back at the house, Brenda had arrived home with Brian.

Sheila greeted him with open arms and Barry, already in his pyjamas, gave him a hearty handshake.

"Do you think we should inform the police that Amelia's back?" Brenda asked.

"What's the point?" Brian interrupted.

"Well, for a start, it would clear your name of her murder! Then there's the minor detail of her already being declared dead!"

Brian smiled at Brenda's sarcasm before plonking himself down in an armchair and allowing his huge legs to spread across the room.

"Well, to be honest, I don't care about being vindicated. I've already done the time for it and it's not like I was totally innocent is it? As for Amelia, I think she ought to stay under the radar for a while. She's got enough going on without the media camping outside to get a look at the new Lazarus!"

"Brian's right." Sheila comforted as she placed her chubby old hand on Brenda's shoulder. "Let's deal with one thing at a time and what matters right now is Frankie and Olivia. They need some quiet time. There will be plenty of time later to decide if we want to set the world alight with this!"

Brenda turned to look into the face of reason. The face of comfort, reassurance and salvation and she thanked God once again for the gift of Sheila.

"Do you think Mealy is telling her?"

"I know she is!" Sheila said firmly. "Wouldn't you want to hear of Amelia's strange collision with some sort of afterlife if you were the one in that sterile bed waiting for the axe to fall?"

Brenda nodded and started to cry.

"Oh love." Sheila held her close. "You have nothing to cry about. You did everything and more for Frankie. You raised her for Amelia with as much love as any mother ever gave to a child."

"No, I didn't." Brenda sobbed. "I tore our family apart. Separated her from her dad and somehow caused her to want a child without a relationship. She slept around and caught that awful disease because of it. Because of me!"

Leigh Oakley

Brian pulled her physically from Sheila's arms into his own.

"None of this is your fault, Bren. If it's anyone's, it's mine."

"And I played my part in the whole thing." Barry interrupted. "I loved that little girl. We had such a lovely relationship, and my stupidity lost her that, on top of the others."

Brenda left the room and returned with a tray of Brandys.

She handed them round and they drank a silent toast to their regrets, their misguided loyalties, their mistakes and failings, their fractured family that had somehow managed to reunite because none of them had ever intentionally damaged or betrayed the other.

"Life is a journey." Sheila added. "A journey full of heartbreak and joy. Of countless decisions with unimaginable consequences and all we can do is to try our best to do what's right. Every one of us has done that. Despite the awful outcomes, we have always done what seemed right."

Each looked to the other and none could find a single example of contradiction.

Sheila smiled and raised her glass. "We have another battle ahead so here's to family."

"To family"

The glasses clinked a new oath and the old regiment prepared themselves for the final battle.

A battle from which one brave, gallant, beautiful soldier would not return home.

Chapter 29

For ten days, Amelia refused to leave Frankie's side.

Brenda brought her fresh clothes and she showered at the hospital, living on sandwiches. At night she slept on a cot bed beside her beautiful daughter and in the day, she watched her sleep, waiting for the moments of lucidity which became rarer and shorter as the days passed.

When Frankie was awake, she would talk to her about their life in the five years they'd been together.

Sometimes they would cry and sometimes they would laugh as Amelia propped her up and inserted the straw into her mouth to allow her to drink a little of the fruit flavoured liquid that was holding her precariously to this world.

The biggest comfort to Frankie was when Amelia would thread their fingers together and sing 'My black cat can play the piano' just as she did when Frankie couldn't sleep as a small child. But now it was saved for the most difficult moments when the pain became too much or the memories too distressing.

In the second week, during one such moment, Frankie suddenly stopped singing and turned to Amelia with wide-eyed fear.

"What is it?" Amelia gasped. "What's wrong?"

"I can't remember what comes next!"

Frankie was staring around her as though the words were hidden somewhere in that room.

"It doesn't matter." Amelia soothed.

"Yes, it does. It matters to me! I used to know that song. I've sung it a million times…My black cat can play the piano, my black cat can play the piano… what comes next? I don't know. Mummy, I don't know it anymore!"

Amelia's heart was breaking as she tried to sing without crying…

"He can play for two and a tanner" she croaked, "kerb or the red brick wall."

Frankie smiled again.

"That's it! That's it."

Amelia, despite everything that had ever happened to her would remember that moment as the worst and most heart-breaking of all. She would never be able to explain why but she would always feel the reason somewhere deep inside her soul. The pure definitive depth of sadness, helplessness and physical, unbearable pain raging through her.

The end was in sight.

From that moment, Amelia rarely ate and refused to take time away to shower or change her clothes.

"Just take a minute or two, please Mealy!" Brenda begged as she handed a fresh set of clothes which Amelia ignored.

"I will stay and watch her for every second you are gone. I promise. You know I will."

Amelia nodded but failed to move.

Brenda had sat in vigil alongside her sister for hours and hours over those days, but she also had Olivia to care for. Sometimes she felt jealous of the devotion Amelia was able to lavish on the woman she'd nurtured for three decades and sometimes she felt like pushing her aside and screaming that Frankie was hers, not Amelia's, but this was no time for animosity or feuding. They were family and they had to pull together and in the same direction.

On occasion, Frankie would open her eyes and see Brenda and a huge smile would light up her face.

"Mum!"

Brenda would kiss her gently and hold her close and that was enough to heal her envy. She knew that in that smile lay 37 years of memories. Of the happy days they'd shared and the endless support and love she'd devoted to her as a child, a teenager, and a woman. Nothing Amelia could do now would ever erase a single moment of it.

That might well have been true, but Amelia was now giving her something that Brenda could not.

In those private moments of lucidity, Amelia was giving her daughter hope.

"I know now, how this works," she said confidently, "I know that although your Grandad died over three decades ago, he will believe that he saw you only a few hours ago."

"But he won't recognise me!"

"Yes, he will. I recognised your voice when you called for me. It didn't sound like the voice of the 5-year-old I remembered but I knew it was you!"

Frankie frowned and Amelia wiped away the beads of sweat that had suddenly appeared on her brow.

"When I was in the car with your father, with Frank I mean. Well, I couldn't so much touch him as feel him. I knew him from some recognition other than touch or sight. I think I could feel the essence of him. It's hard to describe."

She noticed Frankie nodding.

"You know what I mean?"

Frankie nodded again.

"I think I felt you respond when I called for you and I think I felt you approach before I opened my eyes and saw you."

Amelia smiled widely. The comfort she was giving her little girl in these final days was priceless because it represented hope and it offered the promise of a future.

"This isn't the end, Frankie. I promise. Auntie Brenda will be with you again in a matter of hours and I'll be with you before your first day has passed." She then grinned widely, "Sheila will be there before you've even sat down!"

Frankie was trying desperately to accept the concept of it all. The sheer implausibility of it and if it was coming from any other lips than her own mother's she would dismiss it in a heartbeat. She smiled again as she looked on her mother's twenty-two-year-old face and there was no room for doubt.

"I need you to bring up Gilly." She whispered breathlessly.

"Gilly?"

"Olivia." Frankie corrected. "You've a lot better chance of winning the mum's race on sports day than mum has... I mean Auntie Brenda."

Amelia quickly offered her oxygen to combat the breathlessness of the giggle her own joke had invoked.

"Of course, I will take care of my granddaughter. You don't need to worry about that. Brenda and I are a team. We always have been, and we always will be."

"Remember the dress your own mum made for you? The beautiful satin dress you wanted to see me in when I was old enough?"

Amelia took the twist of the knife bravely.

"You mean the one you didn't get to wear because I wasn't there to see it?"

Frankie watched the guilt sadden her face.

"That doesn't matter now. I just want Olivia to be the one to wear it. For your mum, for you and for me. For every stitch of love she made throughout the night"

She noticed the frown on Amelia's face.

"Mum told me all about it. Don't let that love go to waste. No love should ever go to waste."

"I promise." Amelia smiled, brushing away tear after tear until there was no longer any point. She placed both her hands on Frankie's and allowed them to flow unattended.

"Why are you crying?"

Amelia forced another smile.

"It's just that a couple of weeks ago I was sitting on a bus with you." She sobbed for several seconds before regaining her composure. "You were a tiny little thing with a carrier bag in your hand containing the most horrendous rainbow dress and I would give anything to be back there."

Frankie couldn't begin to imagine how that felt.

"Sometimes," Amelia continued, "when I wake up on that cot bed, for a second, I imagine it's all been just a terrible dream. Like the one in Scrooge when he gets the chance to relive his life and put it all right."

Frankie took a breath from the oxygen mask and spoke in small gasps.

"What would you do. If we were back on that bus?"

"I would go straight home with you and stay there. I wish I could go even further back to when Frank found me in the café. I wish I had smiled politely and told him I already had a life and a family. I wish I had never told him he was your father. I already had enough joy for anyone. More than enough!"

"But love isn't like that?" She whispered, reminding Amelia of her previous analogy.

"No. I guess it isn't."

They threaded their fingers again and Amelia tapped out the beat and sang the song as Frankie mouthed the words.

"My black cat can play the piano, he can play for two and a tanner, kerb or the red…"

Frankie's lips became still.

Amelia spoke the final words "brick wall" as her tears fell, and through those tears she could see those beautiful, half-open lifeless eyes that had suddenly turned to glass.

She had watched that beautiful soul enter this world and she had watched it leave again.

She sat with Frankie's hand in hers for over an hour before she called for a nurse. Ignoring the bustling of the ward, the ringing of her phone and the sirens outside until she had waved her little girl goodbye until she was completely out of sight. Just as she had when she was on her way to school with her large satchel almost to her knees. Waving and waving with a fixed smile to disguise the ache in her heart in knowing that her little daughter was striding bravely towards a world she could have no part in.

Eventually she took out her phone and listened to her voicemail.

"Mealy, it's me! Is Frankie alright? I'm worried because Gilly just said she'd seen her mummy. Call me back."

Chapter 30

Amelia's heartache, grief and desolation were swept away in a tidal wave of panic.

She ran down the corridors constantly dialling Brenda, fumbling on the keys from lack of experience and fear.

As she bullied her way into a taxi that someone else had ordered at the door as she heard the phone go to voicemail.

"Bren. It's Mealy. Keep her in your sight. Don't leave her alone. Not for one moment. Frankie has just passed away. Don't let Olivia anywhere near anything that remotely looks or feels like her mummy to her. Ring me back!"

The journey felt endless as Amelia tapped her feet on the mat with one hand firmly on the handle ready to jump out. The brutal way she had delivered the news of Frankie's death to Brenda failed to resonate because this was about Olivia now and her maternal instincts had shifted to the protection of her living offspring. Just as nature intended.

Before they'd even got to the front gate she threw a twenty pound note onto the front seat and held the door ajar with one foot an inch from the ground.

In an instant she was surging through the front door screaming for Brenda.

In the living room Brenda was sitting with her head in her hands sobbing.

"Where's Olivia? Bren? Where's Olivia!"

The door to Sheila's room clicked open and Sheila appeared with Olivia holding her hand.

Amelia's ashen face started to regain a little colour as she flopped into an armchair.

"I thought… I thought…why didn't you answer your phone!"

"Sorry." Brenda replied softly, "It's on charge somewhere."

"What happened?" Amelia gasped.

"Olivia said she saw her mummy." Brenda smiled as she glanced over at the little girl who was also smiling.

"I did see her! She came back to see me when I was in the garden."

Sheila squeezed her hand as Amelia and Brenda exchanged a tense glance.

"Tell Auntie Amelia what happened." Brenda coaxed.

"She just said she had to go away and had come to blow me a kiss."

"Then what happened?"

"I said I wanted a real kiss, but she told me I couldn't because I had to catch it. I caught it. I know I did but then she went away."

"Come on. Let's find you some ice cream." Sheila smiled.

"With a flake?"

"With a flake."

As they left for the kitchen Amelia looked Brenda in the eye.

"She was keeping Olivia at arms-length."

Brenda nodded. "I know. Protecting her. Just like a mother would."

Amelia walked over to Brenda and knelt before her.

"Between us, we created a wonderful human being, Bren."

"The best." Brenda smiled through the tears that were once again, falling faster than she could wipe them.

"I love you more then anyone in the world Bren."

"I love you too. And just look at you! Now it's your turn to be the pretty one."

Amelia reached for Brenda's hairpin and allowed her grey-blonde hair to fall around her shoulders.

"Look at you! You are still the pretty one! You always were. Inside and out!"

They sat together holding hands in complete silence for the longest time. Each drawing comfort and strength from the other and allowing the love to tend their shredded hearts. A million memories, a million heartbreaks and a million unfulfilled dreams passing between them.

Then Amelia stood up.

"Did you keep our old bikes?"

"Of course. What would be the point of buying the house if I didn't have the bikes."

"Want to go for a ride?"

Brenda's shocked expression suddenly turned into the tiny hint of a grin.

"I'm an old woman!"

"Shut up and get the bikes out."

The two women who circled that familiar drive that day before racing out onto the lane towards the old wood, looked like grandma and granddaughter, but inside they were just two little sisters with the wind in their hair, peddling away the pain as they peeled back the years to those happy, carefree days of childhood.

They dumped the bikes halfway down the old track just as they used to as children and ran the rest of the way to the old clearing.

In the undergrowth, the old plastic sheet, now ragged and faded, had waited patiently for them to drag it over the nettles before laying down.

Brenda reached for Mealy's hand as they gazed up into the sky towards the place, they imagined their mother to be waiting for them. Reunited with their dad who would now be holding Frankie in his arms. And of course, where Frank would be finally meeting his beautiful daughter.

Again, no words were spoken as they reminisced on the many, many times they had laid in this spot. Staring through that space in the trees up through the clouds and to the heavens beyond. But today the feeling was so very different. Today they looked not into the unknown but into the known. The place where everyone they loved waited for them to complete their time in this world and join them in the next. The wait that, to them, would feel like no time at all!

Brenda suddenly squeezed her sister's hand to get her attention.

"What?" Amelia asked.

"It's good to have you back."

"It's good to be back, even though I don't feel like I've ever been away."

Brenda propped herself up on her elbow and as the sun caught her skin it emphasized every wrinkle on that wonderful face.

"Want to try something?"

"What?" Amelia asked.

"You think of a colour, and I'll tell you what you're thinking."

"Fuck off!"

Amelia jumped to her feet.

"I was just kidding." Brenda yelled after her.

Amelia was storming away as Brenda watched her go.

"I'm sorry! It was bad taste! I'm sorry!"

"You will be when I beat you home. You've given me a head start now!"

Amelia ran like the wind up that familiar path as Brenda jogged her aged body into a gentle trot.

"I hate you Mealy Gilbert!"

"Back atcha' Amelia called as she peddled away.

Brenda stood breathlessly with her bike still at her feet and watched her sister pedal away as though her life depended on it and in that moment, she knew for certain, that they were going to be alright.

Printed in Great Britain
by Amazon

60829356R00147